Dear Amy,

Thank you again for baby-sitting baby Dexter while I am away. I can't tell you what a comfort it is to me to know that little Dexter will be in good hands. Plus just think, this will be great practice for you when you have your own family....

Also, I know that sharing such intimate quarters with my brother might prove difficult, but it is important to me that baby Dexter remain in familiar surroundings. By the way, while you are playing house with Nick—make sure you don't fall for him. He isn't the marrying kind. On second thought, maybe you are the one woman who can convince the confirmed bachelor to finally take the marriage plunge...!

XOXO Lola

Dear Reader,

Things get off to a great start this month with another wonderful installment in Cathy Gillen Thacker's series THE DEVERAUX LEGACY. In *Their Instant Baby*, a couple comes together to take care of an adorable infant—and must fight *their* instant attraction. Be sure to look for a brand-new Deveraux story from Cathy when *The Heiress*, a Harlequin single title, is released next March.

Judy Christenberry is also up this month with a story readers have been anxiously awaiting. Yes, Russ Randall does finally get his happy ending in *Randall Wedding*, part of the BRIDES FOR BROTHERS series. We also have *Sassy Cinderella* from Kara Lennox, the concluding story in her memorable series HOW TO MARRY A HARDISON. And rounding out things is *Montana Miracle*, a stranded story with a twist from perennial favorite Mary Anne Wilson.

Next month begins a yearlong celebration as Harlequin American Romance commemorates its twentieth anniversary! We'll have tons of your favorite authors with more of their dynamic stories. And we're also launching a brand-new continuity called MILLIONAIRE, MONTANA that is guaranteed to please. Plus, be on the lookout for details of our fabulous and exciting contest!

Enjoy all we have to offer and come back next month to help us celebrate twenty years of home, heart and happiness!

Sincerely,

Melissa Jeglinski
Associate Senior Editor
Harlequin American Romance

# Cathy
# Gillen Thacker

## THEIR
## INSTANT BABY

HARLEQUIN®

TORONTO • NEW YORK • LONDON
AMSTERDAM • PARIS • SYDNEY • HAMBURG
STOCKHOLM • ATHENS • TOKYO • MILAN • MADRID
PRAGUE • WARSAW • BUDAPEST • AUCKLAND

ISBN 0-373-16949-3

THEIR INSTANT BABY

Visit us at www.eHarlequin.com

**Printed in U.S.A.**

# ABOUT THE AUTHOR

Cathy Gillen Thacker married her high school sweetheart and hasn't had a dull moment since. Why, you ask? Well, there were three kids, various pets, any number of automobiles, several moves across the country, his and her careers, and sundry other experiences. But mostly, there was love and friendship and laughter, and lots of experiences she wouldn't trade for the world.

You can find out more about Cathy and her books at www.cathygillenthacker.com, and you can write her c/o Harlequin Books, 300 East 42nd Street, New York, NY 10017.

## Books by Cathy Gillen Thacker

### HARLEQUIN AMERICAN ROMANCE

### HARLEQUIN BOOKS

# Who's Who
## in the Deveraux Family

**Tom Deveraux**—The head of the family and CEO of the Deveraux shipping empire that has been handed down through the generations.

**Grace Deveraux**—Estranged from Tom for years, but back in town—after a personal tragedy—for some much-needed family support.

**Chase Deveraux**—The eldest son, and the biggest playboy in the greater Charleston area.

**Mitch Deveraux**—A chip off the old block and about to double the size of the family business via a business/marriage arrangement.

**Dr. Gabe Deveraux**—The "Goodest" Samaritan around. Any damsels in distress in need of the good doctor's assistance…?

**Amy Deveraux**—The baby sister. She's determined to reunite her parents.

**Winnifred Deveraux Smith**—Tom's widowed sister. The social doyenne of Charleston, she's determined never to marry. That's not what she has in mind for her niece and nephews, though.

**Herry Bowles**—The butler. Distinguished, indispensable and devoted to his boss, Winnifred.

**Eleanor**—The Deveraux ancestor with whom the legacy of ill-fated love began.

# Chapter One

"Look, I don't want to upset your sister—obviously she has enough on her plate right now—but I've got to be honest with you. I don't think this is going to work," Amy Deveraux told Nick Everton the moment she came face-to-face with him on his sister Lola's doorstep. "Not on any twenty-four-hours-a-day, seven-days-a-week basis, anyway."

For once in her life, Amy was going to be practical—instead of emotional. She was going to let her actions be ruled by her head, not her heart. And there was simply no way Amy could share such intimate quarters with this man and the adorable three month old baby Nick cradled awkwardly in his arms.

Forget that Nick Everton was the most drop-dead gorgeous, thirty-six-year-old guy Amy had ever seen. Forget that he was successful, smart, funny—according to Lola, anyway—and genuinely dependable and chivalrous. Or that he was kin to one of her best friends. Nick Everton was just too darn big and physically imposing. Amy guessed he was at least two-hundred and twenty pounds of solid muscle on a six-foot-five frame. His shoulders were broad, his waist trim. And he looked great in his dark-blue suit and slate-blue shirt and tie.

"I thought I was supposed to be the one heading for the hills," Nick said, as he propped a hiccuping Dexter against his shoulder and patted his nephew clumsily on the back. Nick's light-gray eyes gleamed as he took Amy in with the same steady-but-curious appraisal Amy was giving him. "Me, being a guy and all…"

Amy forced her glance away from the wind-tossed strands of Nick's ash-blond hair and ruggedly hand-some face. "So maybe we could just split the baby-sitting duties, fifty-fifty," Amy continued, determined to work this out rationally, in a way that was accept-able to all three of the adults involved.

Nick shrugged. "Sounds good to me," he said, the corners of his masculine lips lifting in an enticing smile.

"There's only one problem with that," Lola inter-rupted as she came out to join them on the raised porch of her South Carolina low-country cottage. She shot an affectionate look at her brother before taking Dexter from him and ushering Nick and Amy inside. "Nick's never baby-sat for Dexter, Amy. You have."

Only once, Amy thought, when Lola'd had a doc-tor's appointment. Dexter had been asleep the entire time. Amy hadn't had to do a thing except watch over the little angel. "Nick and Dexter seem to be getting along now," Amy pointed out as she tried to avoid the tantalizing sandalwood cologne clinging to his skin. Nick might not know much about how to hold a baby, as had been evidenced by his awkwardness with his nephew, but Dexter had cuddled against Nick's powerful shoulders and chest willingly and instinctively.

"Nick also knows nothing about taking care of babies. In fact, it's my guess my brother has never so much as changed a diaper," Lola continued, stating her case matter-of-factly.

Nick shrugged and shoved both hands into the pockets of his trousers. A devilish look on his face, he braced a shoulder against the wall and smiled confidently at both Amy and his younger sister. "How hard can it be?"

Lola merely rolled her eyes. "And Dexter can get really fussy sometimes," Lola continued firmly to Amy. "Nick would definitely have a hard time dealing with that."

Nick grinned at Amy, not about to dispute the veracity of that particular observation. "So maybe it could be your turn then," Nick said to Amy with a wink.

"I'm not kidding around here, Nick," Lola told him sternly, commanding his attention once again. "It's going to be traumatic enough for Dexter to be separated from me indefinitely. He needs both a 'mother' and a 'father' here with him while I'm gone.''

Abruptly Nick straightened and moved away from the wall. His expression was suddenly every bit as serious as his thirty-four-year-old sister's. ''Dexter has a mother and a father, Lola,'' Nick reminded her quietly. He spoke as if carefully underscoring every word. ''He has you and Chuck.''

Lola swallowed, her face suddenly becoming pinched and pale, as the upsetting events of the day— which had started by a visit from military personnel— caught up with her. She began to tremble. ''What if something happens to one or both of us?'' she whispered as she sank onto the nearest chair. ''What happens to Dexter then?'' she asked plaintively.

''Nothing will happen,'' Nick promised her firmly. The tension between the two Evertons climbed.

Lola looked unconvinced as she bounced her baby boy on her thigh. ''You more than anyone ought to know how unpredictable life can be,'' Lola began nervously. ''Sometimes things just happen.''

Like Lola's husband's unexpected injury in the line of duty, Amy thought sympathetically. But Lola's older brother had no such sympathy for his sister, Amy noted, perplexed. Instead of agreeing with Lola, Nick Everton gave Lola a warning look, as if ordering her to say nothing more on that dark subject. More tension flowed between Lola and Nick, and the room fell silent, but for baby Dexter's conversational gurgle. Lola and Nick were still staring at each other when the doorbell rang. Cradling Dexter closer, Lola hurried to the door. "That must be Jack Granger now," she said.

Amy caught Nick's puzzled glance and explained, "I asked Jack to come over. He's a family friend and an attorney, and Lola wanted some papers drawn up before she got on the plane to Germany this afternoon. It's not the kind of work Jack normally does—he's a corporate lawyer for my family's shipping company—but he agreed to help us out because there was literally no other way to get a will drawn up and notarized on such short notice."

"Not to mention the guardianship papers," Jack Granger said as he strode into the room. One of those guys who was all business all the time and not in the least bit emotional, Jack gestured at the woman accompanying him. "Everyone, this is Sue. She's a notary public, and she's going to attest that everything done here today is certified."

Everyone said hello to Sue—a petite brunette with a ready smile—as Jack finished the introductions and began to set up for the document signing.

Amy wondered, Was it her imagination, or did the thirty-two-year-old Jack look even a bit more world-weary than usual today? Certainly he was as neatly and conservatively dressed as always in a white button-down shirt, gray suit and nondescript tie. But beneath the surface, he looked a little harried and distracted. And that wasn't *like* Jack. Normally, nothing threw Jack Granger. He'd had such a tumultuous childhood on the wrong side of the tracks that his adult life, even when fraught with difficulty and stress, seemed easy. Which was, of course, why her father and brothers liked and trusted Jack so much. He never whined and complained. He was simply the guy who was there when you needed him. No questions asked. No demands of his own made.

Nick turned back to Lola with a questioning look. Lola said, ''I want you and Amy to assume care of Dexter if anything happens to Chuck and or to me.''

''Nothing is going to happen to you,'' Amy said quickly.

''I certainly hope that's true,'' Lola said, her pretty face set determinedly, ''but just in case, I want to make sure Dexter has legal documents dictating his care before I take off for Germany. It's better to be safe than sorry. And every parent should have a will, spelling out their child's future, in the event of a tragedy. I've been remiss not getting it done thus far. No longer.''

Amy exchanged glances with Nick. Neither spoke, but it seemed on one point they were in complete agreement. Lola had already had one heck of a day, learning her career-military husband had been injured in a Special Forces mission overseas and flown to Germany for surgery. Right now Chuck was stable, but they weren't sure he would ever walk again, and he needed his wife by his side. Lola had to go. She didn't want to take her baby to the military hospital overseas. So she had asked her best friend, Amy, and her brother to simultaneously care for Dexter in her absence. Both had agreed readily—they wanted to do their part as Dexter's godparents—even if the christening officially naming them as such hadn't taken place yet, and wouldn't until Chuck returned to the States and could be present.

"Okay," Nick said, nodding. "I agree, a will is a good idea. And since Dexter will need both a male and a female presence in his life, in the unlikely event anything happens to both you and Chuck, I'll be glad to step in for you. I assume Amy here feels the same way." Nick looked at Amy.

Her mood suddenly as serious as Nick's, Amy nodded. "I'm honored you've asked me, Lola."

"It seemed right," Lola said quietly. "Since you were my labor coach and here when Dexter came into the world."

"But as for the rest of it," Nick continued gently, speaking to his little sister in a practical, reassuring manner, "that is where and how we care for Dexter in your absence during the next few days or weeks, I agree with Amy—we may need to rethink what you've planned. This house of yours is great, perfect for newlyweds like you and Chuck."

Amy agreed wholeheartedly with that. The cozy country cottage had a combination kitchen, dining and living room, bathroom with claw-foot tub and pedestal sink, a small nursery and an equally tiny master bedroom with only a double bed. "But for two adults like me and Nick who are relative strangers,"

Amy added gently, "the quarters are pretty tight. Even if you include the screened-in back porch. I'd gratefully offer my home as an alternative, but I'm still having the master bathroom remodeled. And the work won't be finished for another three or four days." She couldn't take baby Dexter into that mess, exposing him to construction dust and paint fumes. It wouldn't be safe.

"Maybe we should go to a hotel in Charleston, then," Nick suggested. "Get adjoining private suites."

Amy breathed a sigh of relief. That sounded so much better to her…so much less intimate than the current proposed circumstances!

"I know you can afford it," Lola said, frowning up at her older brother once again. "With all the money you've made producing those syndicated television shows, you're richer than most movie stars, but the answer to that is no, Nick. I stayed with Dexter in a hotel once and he hated it. And he also hated going for an overnight at someone else's house. He knew he was in strange surroundings and he didn't sleep a wink all night."

"Maybe it's time to broaden his horizons," Nick countered amiably.

Lola sent Nick a censuring glance. "No. Dexter stays in his familiar environment. Trust me on this. He's not used to being away from me." Lola teared up again unexpectedly. Her chin quivered as she struggled to get control of her emotions, before she finished in a low, choked voice, "This separation is going to be hard enough on both of us as it is."

Amy saw Lola's point. Dexter was probably going to have a difficult time coping without his mommy, never mind being thrown into a completely unfamiliar environment. "You're right, of course," Amy told Lola gently as she patted her on the shoulder. Amy turned and gave Nick a quelling look—the same kind her mother had given her father before the two had separated and divorced years earlier. "I agree with your sister, Nick. Dexter will do better if we both stay here. And don't worry." Amy turned back to Lola, promising, "Nick and I will manage. We're adults." The important thing was the baby, she thought. They had to do what was right for Dexter.

Nick merely raised a brow, just as Amy's father used to when he felt her mother had made a highly impractical suggestion.

"Well, now, that's settled," Jack Granger said. He laid the papers neatly out on the coffee table and pulled up two chairs—one for himself and one for Sue, his notary. He motioned for Nick, Lola and Amy to sit on the small sofa.

Lola perched on one end, Dexter still cradled in her arms. To give her friend and the baby enough elbow room, Amy had to scoot closer to Nick. He was warm and solid against her. Too warm and solid and male, Amy thought, as another sizzle of awareness swept through her.

"Okay," Jack said, appearing impatient to get on

with it. "Let's have a look at these papers. And I'll explain what they all mean before you sign them."

TWENTY MINUTES LATER, the legalities were taken care of. Lola had gone over the emergency numbers and instructions she was leaving for Dexter's care, and it was time to go. "You're going to miss your plane if we don't hurry," Jack Granger said. He and Sue were driving Lola to the airport. "And there isn't another airline seat available until tomorrow."

"Okay." The tears Lola had been holding welled up and spilled down her pretty cheeks. She bent to kiss Dexter goodbye. "Mommy loves you," she whispered.

Dexter, not sure what was happening, screwed up his little face as if he, too, was about to cry. In an effort to avoid a calamity, Nick tenderly took Dexter from Lola's arms. "Take good care of Chuck," he told his sister in a low, gravelly voice as he cradled the baby awkwardly against his chest. "We'll take good care of Dexter. And call the first chance—hell, every chance—you get. Amy and I want to know how you're doing."

"And you're going to want to know how Dexter is doing, too," Amy said.

Lola nodded. Too choked up for words, Lola kissed her baby one more time, hugged Amy and then Nick, and then rushed, sobbing openly now, out the door. For her infant son, the emotion emanating from his mother was too much. No sooner was she out the door when Dexter let out a wail that could be heard for three counties. Lola started back for the cottage. Jack Granger grabbed the young mother's arm, shook his head and guided her implacably toward his car. Still crying uncontrollably, Lola got in. Dexter continued to wail. The sympathetic tears Amy had been holding back spilled down her cheeks. Nick turned back to Amy. His eyes, too, were suspiciously moist, but all he did was look at both her and Dexter and try to lighten the mood. "Lola was right, you know," he said. "I'm a real novice, so for all our sakes, I hope you know a lot more than I do about taking care of babies."

His joke was exactly what she needed to get herself back on track. Amy drew a deep breath and wiped away her tears with her fingertips. "I know some things. Not everything." And probably, she thought, not nearly enough to make this baby-sitting experience smooth sailing.

"Well, that's still probably more than I know, at least on a practical level." Smiling as if he hadn't a worry in the world, Nick lifted his hand and waved goodbye to his sister. When Jack's car was out of sight, Nick turned back to Amy and shifted Dexter to a football hold. "So which one of us is going to take the first shift?" he asked casually.

Wishing she weren't so physically attracted to Nick, their enforced quarters so small and cozy and hopelessly romantic, Amy raked her teeth across her lower lip. "That depends." She searched his pewter-gray eyes. "Have you really never changed a dia-per?"

Half of his mouth crooked up in an enticing smile. "I've seen it done. Does that count?"

Amy rolled her eyes. She could see this baby-sitting mission was going to be a laugh a minute. Especially if it turned out that Nick wasn't exaggerating his lack of prowess with infants. Amy shrugged and said, "Depends on how handy you are with the tabs on the disposable diapers, I guess."

Nick grinned and waggled his eyebrows at Amy. "There's one way to find out, isn't there?"

NICK WAS PUTTING on a good front, but the bald truth was, his heart was breaking for his sister, too. This whole situation had to be torture for her. Lola loved Chuck every bit as much as Nick had loved Glenna, and Lola's husband having been badly hurt so soon after they'd married and had a child, must be killing his younger sister inside. But there was a difference, Nick warned himself sternly. Lola's child was fine. And though Chuck was very seriously injured, he did have a chance to recover and resume his life. The three of them could still be a family, provided Chuck made it through the surgery ahead of him and went on to recover as fully as they all hoped. Even if Chuck ended up in a wheelchair, his life forever changed, the three of them could be a family.

The same had not been true for Nick.

By the time *he* had found out what had happened,

his fate had been sealed. His happy family life had come to an end. There had been no going back. And his heart and soul had turned to stone. Except where Lola and her family were concerned.

He loved them with every fiber of his being. Because he knew they were all the family he would ever have. He wasn't going through the loss again.

But Amy Deveraux didn't know that, because Lola hadn't told her about Nick's past. And that was the way Nick wanted it. He'd had enough pity to last him a lifetime. What he wanted now was a normal life, and any satisfaction his business dealings could bring him. That was it. That was all.

Unlike Amy Deveraux, who, according to Lola, was still looking for that special man who would turn her life around and make everything new and exciting and wonderful.

The kind of man he could never be again, no matter how much time elapsed.

"Chuck is going to be fine," Nick continued, knowing he had to say something to reassure Amy and Dexter, who was still wailing, as they went into the nursery. Hoping a dry diaper would make Dexter feel better and stop crying, Nick set Dexter down on the changing table just as he had seen Lola do. Keeping one hand firmly on Dexter's middle, Nick reached for a disposable diaper. Also as he had seen Lola do, he opened the clean diaper and slid it beneath Dexter. He ripped open the tabs, saw that Dexter was just wet, and with some difficulty removed the old diaper and dropped it into the plastic-lined diaper pail beside the bed. "Our military doctors are the best in the world. They'll see that he will walk and even run again."

"You don't know that," Amy protested quietly, her worry apparent. She cleaned Dexter's diaper area with a baby wipe, and then sprinkled cornstarch powder on his lower half. "Sometimes families don't get their happily-ever-afters, Nick."

"But Lola and Chuck and Dexter will," Nick said firmly, aware he had no way of promising that. But he also knew it was important the two of them think that way, just the same. Finished fastening the tabs, he picked up Dexter. To his relief, the diaper, with its cartoon figures on the front, stayed in place, albeit somewhat loosely. Nick turned the momentarily subdued Dexter around and saw smaller cartoon figures on his backside. "Well, that's interesting," he said. Before, the bigger cartoon figures had been on the back of Dexter's diaper, the smaller ones on the front.

Amy peered at him from beneath a fringe of long dark eyelashes. "You realize you put that on backwards, don't you?"

Nick shrugged and handed Dexter over to her. "I'm sure you'll agree that's the least of our problems right now."

In fact, the way Nick saw it, his main problem was not going to be which side of the disposable diaper went where, but how he was going to survive a week or more in the company of Dexter's other, very sexy and very beautiful godparent. Nick had been alone with Amy Deveraux for barely five minutes, and already he found himself wanting, quite badly, to take her to bed. Unusual, to say the least. These days when desire hit him, it was usually fleeting and short-lived. He had the feeling that would not be the case with Amy. No, he'd be remembering her pretty face and cloud of dark-mahogany hair for days and weeks to come. Not to mention those wide-set turquoise eyes, narrow elegant nose, high delicate cheekbones, soft luscious lips and cute stubborn chin.

Dexter squirmed and whimpered once again. Amy put him a little higher against her shoulder, so he was able to fuss and look over her shoulder at the room around them simultaneously. As she gently stroked the infant's back with the palm of her hand, Amy looked at Nick curiously. "Do you have any idea when Dexter here last ate?"

Trying not to notice the way Amy's cotton shirt had ridden up above the waistband of her khaki shorts, revealing several inches of flat, sexy abdomen and silky golden skin, Nick shook his head. Tearing his gaze from the slender but curvy figure visible beneath her loose-fitting knee-length shorts, he shifted his weight to ease the pressure at the front of his slacks and said, "He hasn't had a bottle since I've been here, which is at least two hours."

"Then it's probably time for him to be fed again," Amy decided. She walked toward the kitchen, her hips swaying so gently and provocatively as she moved it was all Nick could do not to groan out loud.

Damn, but it was going to be a long week. Doing his best to return his mind to the task at hand, Nick said, "Lola left some breast milk in the door of the fridge. And there's more in the freezer when that runs out."

Amy handed Dexter to Nick, then moved quickly around the kitchen. Referring often to a handwritten set of instructions on the counter, she warmed Dexter's bottle in the microwave, then gave it a good shake and tested the liquid on the back of her wrist. Satisfied, she took the bottle to Nick, who was leaning against the counter with Dexter cradled in one arm. He put the nipple to Dexter's mouth. Dexter spit it out, turned his head away and cried even more loudly.

Nick and Amy's subsequent tries to feed Dexter proved no more successful than the first. It didn't seem to matter if they were sitting or standing, indoors or out. Rocking him or sitting perfectly still. Nick's nephew was having none of it. Probably, Nick thought, because Dexter kept looking up, expecting to see his mommy's face, and instead, saw him or Amy. Bottom line, as far as Dexter was concerned, it wasn't the usual cozy breast-feeding experience he was accustomed to. And he was mighty ticked off about it. Ticked off enough to go on a hunger strike.

"Now what do we do?" Amy asked anxiously, turning her face to Nick.

Nick sighed. He could think of only one solution. "I guess there's no helping it." He looked at Amy seriously. "You're going to have to take off your shirt."

# Chapter Two

Amy was holding Dexter when Nick made his suggestion, and now she stared at Nick, her pulse taking on a rapid jumping beat. "You're joking, right?" He looked so handsome and self-assured, lounging against the back of the sofa with his jacket off, his tie loosened and his shirtsleeves rolled up to just beneath the elbow. So big and strong and undeniably sexy that all sorts of romantic thoughts and fantasies came to mind. Fantasies Amy knew she should not be having!

Nick shook his head, managing to look even more at home at his sister's small country cottage. "Dexter is used to being fed at Lola's breast."

Heat began to center in Amy's chest and move outward in mesmerizing waves. "Well, I can't breastfeed him!" Amy glared at Nick. "I'm not pregnant or nursing. I don't have any milk!"

Nick gave Amy an exceedingly patient look, apparently oblivious to the havoc he was causing in her.

"I know that," he said as he gave her an affable smile and somehow avoided looking at her breasts. "But I was thinking about something that was on a television show I produce—*Nature's Kingdom*. Have you seen it?"

"Yes," Amy said cautiously, aware that being closed in with Nick and the baby this way was putting all her senses in overdrive. Making her wonder what it would be like to have a husband and an infant in her life. She frowned and continued walking Dexter back and forth. "It's wonderful."

"Thanks." His eyes lit with pleasure. "Anyway, they did a show on puppies who'd been separated from their mother. The new owners comforted the puppies by putting a hot-water bottle covered with a towel with the mother's scent on it next to the puppies. They all snuggled up to it instinctively and it worked to comfort them. So," Nick continued, still approaching the problem logically, "I suggest we try to mimic Dexter's usual mealtime experience as best we can. Therefore—" Nick's glance slid over her body, head to toe, warming Amy even further "—since your skin is obviously a lot smoother and silkier and your body a lot, uh, curvier than mine, I suggest you do the actual feeding, at least this first time, as we try to help him with the transition from his mom's breast-feeding." Nick eased Dexter from Amy's arms and cuddled the squalling infant close. "Lola left a robe in the bathroom on a hook on the door."

Aware her knees suddenly were as wobbly and uncertain as the rest of her, Amy eased past Nick and
Dexter. "You really think this will work?"

Nick shrugged and continued holding Dexter awkwardly against his hard-muscled chest. "I wouldn't
have suggested it if I didn't."

Had they been anywhere else, doing anything else,
Amy would have told Nick Everton exactly what he
could do with his suggestion that she appear in a state
of undress in his presence. But unable to bear Dexter's hiccupy sobs a second longer, Amy slipped into
the bathroom and did as Nick proposed, pulling off
her lemon-yellow shirt and donning the robe. When
she came back out, Nick was standing next to the
rocking chair, Dexter in his arms. His eyes seemed to
darken at the sight of her, and he motioned her to sit.

Her mouth dry, Amy did.

Nick leaned down and put Dexter in Amy's arms.
With fingers that trembled, Amy tried to discreetly
open her robe. Given the way Dexter was still flailing
his little limbs and crying, it was impossible to hold
on to him and do that simultaneously.

Realizing she was attempting an impossible task,
Nick rushed to the rescue. "Hang on. I'll help you,"
he said, regarding her matter-of-factly. He parted the
terry-cloth lapels, revealing Amy's throat and neck,
and the uppermost curves of her breasts above the
lacy transparent demi-bra. There was a moment of
awareness between Nick and Amy as she noted he
had just seen everything there was to see. Flushing,

Amy turned her attention away from her tautening nipples and the rapacious gleam in Nick's eyes, and back to the baby. Still attempting to soothe Dexter, she used both her hands to cuddle the infant close to her and settle his head against her chest.

Amy saw immediately that Nick had been right about one thing. As soon as Dexter's head contacted the soft upper swell of Amy's breast and the feel of her bare skin, he paused, blinking, his tears soaking through to her bra. And although he had stopped crying uncontrollably, Dexter still seemed confused.

"I don't think he knows what to do," Amy murmured.

"Then I'll show him," Nick said softly, gallantly ignoring the way Amy's lacy demi-bra was now clinging wetly to her breast.

His touch both incredibly comforting and precise, Nick leaned down and guided the baby bottle to the infant's mouth once again, murmuring soothingly all the while. Dexter blinked and looked up at Nick with his big, baby blues then sucked on the bottle half-heartedly, a suspicious look on his cherubic face. Nick backed away, still murmuring soothing words, and then three-month-old Dexter looked up at Amy again and began to drink from his bottle in earnest.

Amy, who'd been baby-sitting from the age of twelve, took it from there, while Nick grabbed his cell phone and laptop computer and stepped out to the screened-in porch to do a little business and check for messages. Not once did he turn back and look at Amy and Dexter, and for that, Amy was very glad. She was still unbearably aroused from the close, albeit meaningless contact with Nick, and she didn't want to know if he felt the same potent physical attraction. Because Amy wasn't looking for a fling. She was looking for a deeply satisfying relationship of the heart. One that led to marriage and children of her own. Lola had said little to Amy about her older brother except that she adored him and despaired that Nick's future did not and never would include marriage and kids.

Which of course immediately struck him off Amy's list, despite any attraction she felt for the sexy single man.

Twenty minutes later Dexter had finished the bottle of Lola's breast milk and was sleeping soundly in Amy's arms. Figuring she had better put him in his crib to finish out his nap while she could, Amy stood ever so slowly up with the baby in her arms and made her way cautiously to the nursery. She placed Dexter on his back in the crib, then went to change out of Lola's robe and into the yellow shirt.

Apparently finished with his business calls and e-mail, Nick was waiting for her when she came back out to the living room, a worried look on his face. "What's wrong?" Amy asked immediately, not really all that sure she wanted to hear the answer. She and Nick had been baby-sitting his nephew for only an hour or so, and already she was exhausted from simultaneously trying to do right by Dexter and fight her attraction to Nick. She couldn't imagine how she would feel by the time Lola and Chuck returned, if this kind of emotional whirlwind kept up.

Nick inclined his head in the direction of the kitchen. "By my calculations, there're only a few days' worth of breast milk in Lola's freezer."

"We can buy formula at the grocery store and use that until Lola gets back." Amy paused at the concern on his face. "You don't think Dexter's going to like it, do you."

"Probably not, but we'll cross that bridge when we come to it. The more pressing question at the moment is—" he held her gaze "—how the three of us are going to manage in such tight quarters."

Amy told herself it was tension causing her heart to pound and her mouth to go dry, not his proximity. "I think it'll be okay," she fibbed as she brushed past him and headed for the refrigerator. Ignoring his frank appraisal of her as they talked, Amy pulled out a cold can of vegetable juice and popped the top. Right about now, she could use a healthy pick-me-up. Anything to calm her nerves and make the overall situation seem more manageable. "After all—" Amy continued, trying not to feel self-conscious in her snug-fitting, long-sleeved yellow shirt with the Amy's Complete Redecorating Service logo, khaki shorts, sneakers and socks "—it's not like you and I are going to be with each other twenty-four hours a day." She offered Nick a bracing smile. "I am still going to have to go to work." Which would offer a lot of personal satisfaction, as well as distraction from Nick's sexy presence. "And Lola said you are going to be conducting some business here in Charleston, too."

Nick's expression turned thoughtful as his gaze continued to drift over her hair, face and lips with disturbing thoroughness before returning to her eyes. "That's right," he said, moving closer, every inch of him the hard, indomitable male. "I have an idea for a new syndicated television show I want to pursue."

Amy took another swallow of chilled vegetable juice. "And I have a decorating job that has to be done right away for my aunt Winnifred." Amy was embarrassed to feel a little excess juice on the corners of her lips. She paused to wipe it off with her fingertips, damning the fact that Nick had noticed—and tracked—that movement, too. "So most likely, you'll be here with Dexter while I'm off doing my thing," Amy continued with an airy confidence she didn't begin to feel, "and then I'll be here with him while you're off doing your thing." During the day, they could rarely, if ever, cross paths, Amy reassured herself optimistically, as she took another long, bracing swallow of juice. If she was lucky, she continued bolstering herself firmly, and Nick's work included some evening jaunts, the same would be true of the majority of their nights, as well.

"Actually, speaking of work…there's something you could help me with," Nick said, a hopeful expression on his face.

Amy's brow furrowed at the abrupt change in Nick's mood. She didn't know anything about producing television shows. "What?" she asked him curiously, as she glanced into the utility area on the back porch to see if a load of wash was done. It wasn't.

Nick flashed her a winning smile and focused on her flushed face and tousled hair. "Like getting me an introduction to your mother right away."

NICK SAW AMY'S SMILE fade and her eyes go dark almost instantaneously. Then and there he knew he'd made a mistake. "My mother has an agent who handles queries," Amy said.

"Her agent isn't returning any calls about any opportunities right now," Nick said.

Hectic color filled Amy's cheeks as she folded her arms defiantly. "That's because my mother doesn't want to work right now," Amy explained with exaggerated patience.

Nick moved closer, ignoring the apple-blossom fragrance clinging to Amy's dark, tousled hair and golden skin. This was no time to be noticing how sexy her slim legs were, or how bare, or wondering how they would feel wrapped around his waist. Amy was his sister's best friend, Dexter's other godparent, for heaven's sake. Not to mention the daughter of a television superstar he would very much like to do business with. He couldn't afford to get sidetracked by a lust that was likely to be as short-lived as his time in South Carolina. He didn't need to be recalling how beautiful and full and enticing her breasts were beneath the transparent lace of her low-cut bra, not unless he wanted to forget everything important and concentrate on getting her into his arms and into his bed.

"Which is why," Amy continued with a haughty toss of her hair, exasperation tinging her low voice, "my mother came home to Charleston. She doesn't want to be bothered by you and every other relentless television executive, bent on getting her to listen to his or her pitch of what she should do next. She wants to take her time, relax first, recuperate from her years and years of getting up every morning at 3:00 a.m., before moving on to the next phase of her life."

Nick could imagine there were other reasons Grace Deveraux had gone into seclusion. Grace's being fired from one of the network morning news and entertainment programs in New York City had been both humiliating and unexpected—at least as far as the viewing public was concerned. Grace had been a fixture in homes across America for the past fifteen years. People had watched her as they drank their morning coffee, dressed for work and got their kids ready for school. Finding out the network had given Grace and her equally popular male cohost at *Rise and Shine, America!* the ax had infuriated the duo's many fans.

What Grace obviously hadn't realized, however, was that this was no time for her to go into hiding. With sentiment so strong, now was the time for her to move on. And Nick knew this with every ounce of business acumen he possessed. "All I want is a few moments of your mother's time," he persisted, as aware that he was further infuriating and disappointing Grace's daughter as he was that business was the one pleasure left in his life.

Amy glared at him. "So, call her agent again."

Nick studied her. Was it his imagination, or did Amy have the ripest, most kissable lips he had ever seen? The softest, most feminine hands? "You resent me for even asking you to do this, don't you?"

Amy's expression turned fiercely independent and protective once again as she set her empty can aside, leaned back against the kitchen counter and braced her hands on either side of her. "What do you think?"

Nick shrugged and moved a bit closer. A little show of temper was not going to deter him. Ignoring the feelings of desire generated by her proximity, he continued his honest appraisal of her actions in an effort to bring her around to what was best here, not just for him, but for all concerned. "I think," he told her calmly, ignoring the flash of resentment in those turquoise eyes, "that you don't have your mother's best interests at heart."

Amy released a short, impatient breath and continued to hold his eyes like a warrior princess in battle. "Maybe it's in my mother's best interest *not* to talk to you," Amy shot back fiercely, oblivious to how the way she was standing lifted her breasts and pulled her shirt even more tightly across her alluring curves.

Nick studied her upturned face. "You're telling me Grace is happy, letting her television career end this way?"

"She hasn't said it's over," Amy countered stiffly.

Deciding it was better to tell it like it was than spare Amy and her mother's feelings at this point, he warned point-blank, "Your mother's career will take yet another brutal blow if she doesn't take advantage of the public sentiment in her favor right now. Sure, your mother can wait six months or a year, but the viewing public tends to have a very short attention span. In that amount of time, the momentum she has now will have faded. Her choices will be far fewer. I don't want to see that happen to her." Especially, Nick thought, given how hard Grace Deveraux had worked to get where she was today. "Do you?"

Finally Nick'd hit a nerve with Amy. She realized he was telling her the truth. She pressed her lips together. "Why do you care so much?"

Nick shrugged, the answer simple. "Because I'm in the business of producing television shows for syndication. And I want your mother to have the kind of recognition and opportunity she's due."

Amy sighed in exasperation and shook her head. She turned her glance away from Nick as the washer abruptly stopped running. "I thought my days of dealing with this were over." Amy went out to the washer, which was located against the wall on the screened-in back porch, and lifted the lid.

Nick followed her. "What do you mean?"

Amy hooked a foot around a wicker basket on the floor and tugged it closer to the machine. She reached into the tub and began pulling out damp bed linens, pausing to grimace as the sheet got hopelessly wrapped around the agitator in the center, before asking rhetorically, "Do you have any idea what it was like for me growing up? I couldn't go anywhere or do anything without someone asking me for a favor related to my mother!" New color—whether from anger or exertion, Nick couldn't tell—flooded Amy's cheeks as she flung the first handful of wet laundry into the basket on the floor. As she went back up on tiptoe and reached deep into the tub of the machine, Amy's shorts rode higher, giving him a glimpse of her smooth, silky thighs.

Still unaware of the effect she was having on him, Amy drew a deep aggravated breath and continued enlightening Nick. "My Girl Scout leader wanted to know if our troop could get on the network news show to promote our annual cookie sale. The private high school I attended wanted to do a fund-raiser for a new gymnasium with my mother as the main draw. Even my first clients in the redecorating business called me only because they thought they might somehow get an *in* with my mother."

Nick sympathized with Amy as he reached over to help her extract the wet tangled laundry. "I expect it is hard, having a famous parent." Especially for someone who seemed to feel things as deeply as Amy did. Amy would not have simply been able to blow off being taken advantage of. No, she would have felt it deeply, and continued hurting over it, for years.

"But a lot of people would have given anything to be in your shoes," Nick continued.

"The feeling was mutual, believe me," Amy said as she plucked a mesh bag full of wooden clothespins from the shelf above the drier.

They regarded each other in tense silence. Then Amy picked up the basket and carried it toward the door that led to the backyard. His innate gallantry coming to the fore, Nick took the basket, leaving her with just the mesh bag of pins, and moved ahead to hold the door for her. "I don't suppose your parents were famous," Amy said.

Nick shook his head as he set the basket down on the grass and picked a pillowcase off the laundry pile. He shook it out, then handed it to Amy and watched as she pinned it to the clothesline. "They were—are—Gypsy souls who had no interest in settling down or sticking with anything for very long," Nick said.

Amy accepted a second pillowcase from Nick. "Where are they now?"

Nick shrugged, his face becoming closed, unreadable. "Neither Lola nor I know," he replied, trying not to feel embarrassed about that as he put the best spin he could on the untenable situation. "The last Lola and I heard, which was about two years ago, our folks were traveling around Europe, working whenever, wherever the spirit moved them."

Amy's eyes widened as Nick handed her one end of a damp bottom sheet. "They don't keep in touch?"

Nick shook his head as he and Amy shook out the wrinkles in the sheet and then hung it neatly on the clothesline. "They don't even know Lola had a baby." Which was, Nick ruminated, something that had hurt his younger sister tremendously. But he also knew that had he and Lola managed to track down their parents and tell them the news, and then the nomadic pair decided not to come to see the baby, just as they had earlier refused to return to the States and meet Lola's husband-to-be or attend her wedding, his sister would have been hurt even more. So he and Lola had mutually agreed to leave well enough alone this time and just see their parents when—and if—their parents wanted to see them. You can't get blood from a stone...and you couldn't get familial love from parents who had none to give.

"But you and Lola are close," Amy said as Nick handed her the final sheet.

Nick nodded, very glad about that. "We've always taken care of each other," he said. It was through his relationship with his sister that he had learned how to love and nurture, and be loved and nurtured in return.

"She's lucky she has you."

"And I her," Nick said. And he meant it.

"But back to your mother..." And that introduction he wanted.

"The answer is still no," Amy said.

Nick shrugged, not really surprised, given Amy's

feelings about people using her familial connections as an in—to anyone. He smiled, not the least deterred. "Then I guess I'll have to find another way to achieve what I want, won't I?" he said.

## Chapter Three

While Dexter napped and Nick worked out of his sister's cottage, Amy headed for her afternoon appointment. As usual, her aunt's handsome British butler, Harry Bowles, answered the door. Harry had been with Winnifred since shortly after Winnifred's husband had been killed. He and Winnifred were so close they could read each other's mind. In Amy's estimation, only two things kept them apart. Harry's age—he was five years younger than Winnifred—and Harry's station in life. He had spent his entire adult life working for the wealthy. She was one of those to-the-manor-born. If the two did decide to run off together someday, as Amy suspected both Harry and her aunt Winnifred had at one time or another been tempted to do, the repercussions would continue for years. Because if there was one thing the residents of Charleston, South Carolina, loved, it was a good love story—or a scandal. As had been evidenced by the retelling of her long-lost great-aunt Eleanor's romantic debacle, that had been fodder for the gossips for years. And thanks to the sudden reemergence of the long-presumed-dead Eleanor Deveraux just the week before, it still was.

Amy breezed through the portal of the historic mansion in time to see her beloved aunt emerge from the front parlor. Pretty and elegantly dressed as always, the social doyenne of Charleston glided toward Amy, her arms outstretched, as Harry excused himself wordlessly and disappeared.

Amy paused to hug the dark-haired woman. "Hi, Aunt Winnifred," Amy said, aware that, as always, just being with her aunt made her happy.

"Amy, darling—" Winnifred squeezed her back affectionately "—I'm so glad you could fit us in this quickly."

"Where's Great-Aunt Eleanor?" Amy asked as she shifted her oversize canvas briefcase from her shoulder to her hands. Eleanor Deveraux was the reason for Amy's visit. The elegant eighty-year-old woman had been found in the historic district, with a sprained ankle, delirium related confusion, brought on by her fever and illness, and the beginnings of pneumonia, and admitted to Charleston Hospital by Amy's brother, Gabe, a critical-care doctor there. At the time, no one in the Deveraux family had any inkling that the genteel elderly Jane Doe was related to them. Nor had they known, until Eleanor's identity was revealed by Charleston private investigator Harlan Decker, that Eleanor Deveraux was still alive—since everyone had been told Eleanor had died of a broken heart many years before. As Eleanor had recovered and begun to trust them, the mental confusion that they had first mistaken for amnesia had lifted, and Eleanor finally acknowledged her true identity, shocking everyone.

"Has she stopped resisting the idea of letting us take care of her permanently?" Amy asked. Although she had few choices, Eleanor had been adamant about not being a burden to her relatives.

Winnifred shook her head, looking distressed. "I'm hoping if Eleanor stays here long enough, she'll let me take care of her from here on out. But right now," Winnifred confessed sadly, "she's only agreed to stay until her ankle heals enough for her to get around on her own again."

Aunt Winnifred led the way to the servants' quarters, which were the only bedrooms on the first floor.

The door to one tiny room was open. Harry was seated in a chair next to the narrow bed.

"So this is where you disappeared to," Amy teased. She'd wondered where Harry had been off to in such a hurry. Usually he hung around to talk a little with her, too.

Harry winked at Amy. "Rude of me, I know, but I had some serious business to attend to."

"So I see," Amy murmured back just as playfully, while Winnifred grinned, shaking her head at what was still going on.

Harry was holding a hand of playing cards. Eleanor was propped up against the pillows. Her silver hair coiled atop her head, she was wearing one of Winnifred's elegant satin bed jackets. Eleanor's color was better than the last time Amy had stopped by to see her, at the hospital, but you could still tell from the gaunt angles of Eleanor's face that she had been sick.

Eleanor smiled at Amy and Winnifred, then turned her attention back to Harry. Spreading her cards out in front of her, she announced triumphantly, "Gin!"

Harry shook his head ruefully, then shot Eleanor an admiring glance. "You really must tell me your secret someday."

Eleanor smiled coyly and remained mum.

Harry stood and looked at Winnifred. "Tea and cookies for three?" he asked formally as he straightened his tie.

"Thank you, Harry." Winnifred smiled as she pulled up another chair beside the bed and motioned for Amy to sit in the one Harry had vacated. "That would be lovely."

Once again all business, Harry exited quietly. But Amy wasn't fooled. She had seen the brief but intimate looks he and her aunt Winnifred had given each other. There was more going on between them than they wanted anyone to know, or she would eat her shoe.

"I've asked Amy to help us redecorate your new quarters to your liking," Winnifred told Eleanor.

Eleanor's eyes took on a troubled gleam and she held up a staying hand. "My dear Winnifred, I've told you that redecorating the carriage house on my behalf isn't necessary. This room is lovely and I'm not planning to be here that long. Just another few days.''

It was also claustrophic, Amy thought, looking at the windowless walls. So much so that no one had slept in any of the little rooms of the servants' quarters for years. Even Harry had quarters upstairs on the second floor.

"Where are you going to go?" Winnifred asked plaintively. "You're supposed to stay off your feet as much as possible until your ankle heals completely, and Gabe said that will be another week at the very least."

Eleanor was silent. She turned her glance to the wheelchair and walker next to her bed, then looked down at the ice-blue damask coverlet across her lap. "I think I've brought enough hardship to this family already, without adding any more," Eleanor said in her cultured voice.

"If you're talking about what happened years ago," Amy returned gently, "everyone in the family has agreed it doesn't matter to any of us what happened then."

"I don't know how you can say that." Eleanor speared Amy with a troubled gaze. "I was involved in an illicit love affair. I brought shame to the family name and caused the death of someone I loved very much. My entire family was miserable in the wake of the tragedy, and everyone blamed me."

"If you're talking about the curse Dolly Lancaster

hired a Gypsy to put on you and Captain Nyquist—''
Amy said, but was interrupted by Eleanor.

"As well as the entire Deveraux family! There
hasn't been a happy marriage or an enduring relationship since." Eleanor looked at Winnifred. "Your
husband died within a year of your marriage. Grace
and Tom divorced."

"But the streak of bad romantic luck seems to be
turning around at long last," Amy was all too happy
to point out as she leaned forward urgently. "Chase
married Bridgett, Mitch married Lauren and Gabe
married Maggie. I'm the only one of my parents children left unattached."

"And that is going to change, too," Eleanor promised.

Amy smiled. Her great-aunt had been encouraging
romance—secretly—for years. They had just thought
it was either her ghost or someone pretending to be
her, who had been doing the matchmaking for the
Deveraux heirs. Amy narrowed her eyes at Eleanor.
"How do you know?" she asked.

Eleanor lifted one delicate hand. "Lately I've just
had a knack for predicting such things," Eleanor said.

"Or a knack for matchmaking," Winnifred
amended dryly. Winnifred looked at Eleanor. "That
was you, wasn't it, who was leaving the notes and
sneaking in and out of both my home here and the
Gathering Street mansion where you and Douglas Nyquist used to meet."

Eleanor blushed, looking guilty as charged. "Even

though I was no longer part of the family," she explained sweetly, "I've always tried to keep watch over the entire Deveraux clan."

"I understand why you would want to be close to family," Amy ventured, figuring now was as good a time as any to get all her queries answered. She looked at her great-aunt closely. "What I don't understand is why you let everyone believe you were dead all these years."

Eleanor shrugged and twin spots of color appeared in her cheeks. "It seemed easier for me to disappear and be on my own than to have everyone else linked to the debacle flee Charleston in mortification." Eleanor paused, tears of remorse glistening in her faded-blue eyes. "I thought my 'death' would end the misery, but it didn't. The scandal only seemed to get worse. And since I made my mistakes, no one connected to me who stayed in Charleston has remained unscathed. That's why I stayed away from the family all these years. And would have continued to do so, had I not gotten hurt and you not figured out who I was. Because that was how I thought I could best protect the rest of you from the pain I had already suffered."

Amy thought Eleanor's motives had been noble, if misguided. "But now the secret's out," Amy said pragmatically, "don't you think you should stay with us from now on?"

"I don't want to be a burden," Eleanor said simply as Harry came back into the room carrying a large tray with a silver tea service and several plates of snacks.

"Your money is gone?" Winnifred guessed.

Eleanor nodded reluctantly, the embarrassed color in her cheeks deepening. "I have less than a thousand dollars in the bank, which is why I have to leave as soon as possible."

"To go where?" Winnifred asked, plainly vexed. "And do what?"

Eleanor shrugged and averted her eyes. "I'll get by."

"You need to do more than that," Winnifred said sternly. "You need a job."

Amy gaped at her aunt Winnifred. As did Eleanor. What could an eighty-year-old woman with a bum ankle do? But clearly, the fifty-year-old Winnifred had plans.

"I'm in need of a good social secretary," Winnifred said firmly, apparently not about to take no for an answer. "So, Eleanor, how's your penmanship?"

IN SHORT ORDER, it was agreed that Eleanor would stay on indefinitely with Winnifred and hand-address the invitations and place cards for Winnifred's many parties in exchange for her room and board. The long-unused carriage house behind Winnifred's mansion would provide sleeping quarters and an office for Eleanor.

"I've been meaning to make the carriage house into a guest house for years, anyway," Winnifred said airily as she and Amy entered the old structure, which had been used for storing her antiques.

"Why haven't you?" Amy asked.

Abruptly Winnifred looked very sad. "Because I didn't want anyone here. This was where my husband and I stayed when we were newlyweds, before he went off to serve overseas."

Winnifred's husband had been killed a year into their marriage. She had lived with her parents in the carriage house until they had died and then moved into the mansion. "But it's time it became something other than a source of my memories," Winnifred said thoughtfully.

"Does this mean you're ready to move on—romantically, too?" Amy asked.

Winnifred's expression became closed. "I'll never marry again," she said. "You know that."

Except, Amy thought, if she was correct in her observations, her aunt already loved someone—Harry—even if Winnifred wouldn't yet admit it to herself. "So," Amy said, getting out her notepad as she realized time was really getting away from her. She was supposed to be back at the cottage in less than an hour, as per her baby-sitting agreement with Nick. She smiled at Winnifred. "What did you have in mind?"

DEXTER WOKE UP grumpy from his nap, and he stayed grumpy, no matter what Nick did. Although Nick had gotten lucky when he'd figured out how Dexter, who was used to being breast-fed, might want to take his bottle, he had no idea what to do with a cranky baby who'd already had a nap, had his diaper changed and had no interest in eating again yet. So Nick tried to remember some of the tips he'd seen on various television shows he'd produced.

He walked Dexter outside. He rocked him inside. He sang to him. He cuddled him. He put him down on a soft blanket on the floor. He waved toys in front of his face. He made silly sounds, even sillier faces. He soothed, he pleaded, he begged until he was up and walking the floors with the baby and close to shedding a few tears himself.

And it was then, Nick noted with resentment and relief, that Amy walked in the front door. She was lugging her canvas briefcase and several large wallpaper and carpet sample books. She looked harried and tired, and it was quickly apparent from the indignant scowl on her face that she blamed Nick for Dexter's crying spell. Dropping her belongings in a heap, she rushed to Dexter and scooped him out of Nick's arms.

Dexter quieted immediately as he gazed adoringly into Amy's face. Nick didn't know whether to be consoled or annoyed that she so easily did what he had just spent more than an hour trying to accomplish. "Obviously he likes you more," Nick said with a sigh, recalling—without wanting to—a similar situation in which he had failed a child, badly. Nick clenched his jaw. "So maybe you should take care of him from now on.'' Judging by the way his nephew was behaving, it would certainly be better for Dexter.

Amy's chin jutted out stubbornly. She angled her head at him, looking both pretty and furious. "I don't think so," she said.

"You can see I'm lousy at it," Nick argued, feeling exasperated. For reasons that were both egotistical and familial, he might not want to be honest in his assessment of his abilities regarding child care—but for all concerned, he knew he had to be. He couldn't afford to let Dexter down, especially with Lola and Chuck both overseas. Giving his nephew the best possible care was the least Nick could do under the circumstances.

"Oh, pshaw. That's a lame excuse if ever I heard one," Amy said as she walked Dexter back and forth.

Nick tried not to notice the intuitive way she had cuddled Dexter against the pillowy softness of her breasts, or how gently and tenderly she held him. No doubt about it, Amy would make an excellent—and very loving and caring—mother. With effort he returned his gaze to Amy's face and struggled to keep his mind on the subject at hand. "I beg your pardon?"

Amy pursed her lips and continued to regard him contentiously. "Guys always say things like that to get out of doing things around the house or with their kids," she told him disparagingly. "I see it all the time with my married friends, and I have to tell you—" Amy paused and looked him straight in the eye "—it infuriates me."

Nick braced a shoulder against the wall and returned her steady gaze. "Dexter's been crying for an hour. I've done everything possible to quiet him, with no result. You waltz in—a good forty-five minutes later than you said you would be, by the way—you glare at me, take him from me, and bingo, the kid is happy as can be." What did she call that if not proof that Nick was not exactly material for Stand in Father of the Year? Never mind husband or father material—for anyone. Pain twisting his gut at the loss he had suffered in the past and the emptiness and loneliness that would no doubt be part of his future, Nick swallowed hard and forced himself to stand up to the quiet accusation in Amy Deveraux's turquoise eyes. "My nephew knows what he wants and what he wants is you," Nick said gruffly, irritated at finding himself failing so completely and unexpectedly again. He looked at Dexter's tearstained face. "Believe me, he couldn't have been clearer about *that*." And that hurt, too. Because even though the two of them hadn't yet spent much time together, Nick loved his nephew, Dexter, as much as he loved his sister, Lola. He hadn't expected to be so summarily rejected the first chance the two of them had been alone together. But he had been, Nick thought, discouraged and exhausted. There was no denying that.

"Nonsense. He's simply confused and missing his mommy." Amy cuddled Dexter close and smoothed

Dexter's down hair with gentle, maternal strokes. "All he wanted was to be comforted."

"I did comfort him!"

Amy merely lifted a brow. Nick could see she didn't believe him.

"Honestly—" Nick lowered his voice with effort and put the overwhelming emotion he felt aside "—I did my best. And it wasn't good enough."

Nick looked at Amy sternly, knowing she was probably going to fight him on this, but knowing also there was no other choice, he laid down the law. "No more going our separate ways. You're going to have to stay with me and Dexter from now on. At least until Dexter adjusts to his mother's absence."

*Chapter Four*

Amy would have thought Nick was just trying to wriggle out of the promise he had made to his sister to look after her son had she not seen the anguish on Nick's face. He truly was out of his league here—or so he thought. And a man like Nick did not want to be in a situation where he could possibly fail.

"You're being ridiculous," she said in no uncertain terms.

"Look, Amy, I wish it were otherwise, but the bottom line is I don't have the instinct for something like this. Never have had and never will."

He wasn't as bad at it as he thought. After all, she had seen Nick change Dexter's diaper and hold him earlier without any problem. Initially Dexter had snuggled against Nick's broad, sinewy chest every bit as readily as he had cuddled against the softness of her breasts. But apparently Nick had gained no confidence from that.

"So what are you saying?" Amy asked, doing her

best not to let how handsome Nick looked in the fading afternoon light distract her. While she had been gone, he had changed into faded jeans and a dark-gray polo shirt that made the most of his tall, muscular frame. His hair was mussed, as if he'd run his hands through it, and the hint of evening beard gave him a mesmerizingly sexy I'm-in-charge-here look. Swallowing hard around the sudden tightness in her throat, she stepped back. "That you're not willing to do your part in taking care of Dexter from here on out?"

"No." Nick's glance drifted over her in a decidedly sensual appraisal, lingering on the close fit of the sleeveless rose-colored blouse and matching tea-length skirt she had changed into before going over to her aunt's, then returning to her face. His voice lowered to a hushed, seductive murmur that did nothing to disturb the drowsy baby in her arms. "I'm telling you that until Dexter adjusts to the two of us taking care of him, you should be close enough to comfort him if he needs it—just like you're doing now."

His plan sounded practical. Romantic even, if Amy contemplated the notion of being tucked away in decidedly intimate and cozy surroundings with a baby she was fast coming to adore and a handsome man. There was only one problem, she thought, aside from her very physical attraction to Nick and the fact that she wasn't the type of woman who would ever have a fling.

"What about my work?" Amy said seriously. And although she didn't want to let Dexter, Nick or Lola down, she had professional commitments. Her word was her bond. She couldn't just walk away from that.

He regarded her seriously, suddenly looking as enamored of her as she was of him. "I respect that," he said with a persuasive smile, "but I'm sure with some judicious planning, the two of us can both manage to get our jobs done and care for Dexter. Even if that means, in the short run, that Dexter and I go where you go."

Amy contemplated that as a sizzle of awareness swept through her slender five-foot-seven frame. She wasn't sure how much she could actually accomplish with Nick Everton underfoot—his sexy presence was a pretty potent distraction. On the other hand, she didn't want Dexter to be crying inconsolably again just because he'd awoken from a nap and didn't have either his mommy or a similarly female presence there to comfort him. Plus, she could see Nick was just trying to do what was best for his nephew, even if that meant he had to admit his inadequacy, something she figured the successful executive did not have an easy time doing. Nick was the kind of man who wanted to succeed at literally everything.

"All right," Amy said after a moment, figuring this really was for the best. "I'll make sure I'm with the two of you until we know Dexter has adjusted to us being here, instead of Lola."

"Thanks," Nick said with a relieved smile.

Aware of how easy it would be to get intimately involved here—with both Dexter and Nick—Amy looked down and saw that Dexter had gone to sleep again. Knowing she had to get the infant settled, Amy put Dexter down in his crib, covered him with a blanket and went back to the living room. "I promised my aunt I'd have a proposal ready for her by tomorrow morning, so I've got to get busy on it while Dexter is sleeping," she said.

Nick nodded. "I'll run to the grocery for us while you're working. And pick up some dinner and anything else you'd like while I'm out." He paused. "Do you need anything?"

"No," Amy said, figuring the time apart would do them good, help her stop having these…thoughts. "Thanks."

Amy waited until Nick had left, then sighed and went back out to her car. She brought in the card table, printer, digital camera, her laptop computer, a ream of paper and a corkboard and stand. She set up quickly and quietly, then kicked off her sandals and got down to work. To her relief, Dexter continued sleeping and was still sleeping when Nick returned, a little over an hour later. He came in carrying two bags of groceries in one arm and a big sack of Sticky Fingers carry-out in the other. Amy couldn't suppress a delighted smile as she inhaled the delicious flavors of her favorite South Carolina barbecue. Maybe, she thought, sharing quarters with Nick and the baby wouldn't be so difficult, after all.

Amy set the table while Nick put the milk, orange juice, eggs, bacon, bread, coffee and disposable diapers away. Together they opened up the barbecue sacks. "I wasn't sure what you liked, so I got a little of everything," he said.

He sure had, Amy noted happily. There were containers of hickory-smoked barbecued pork ribs, smoked turkey and rotisserie chicken. Barbecued baked beans, homemade coleslaw and potato salad, cinnamon baked apples, dirty rice, even some frog-more stew. His expression perplexed, Nick pointed to the container. "I wasn't quite sure what this was," he said, taking the lid off the spicy mixture. "But they assured me it had no frog in it. Just potatoes, peppers, onions, corn, sausage, shrimp and their special blend of spices."

"It's actually pretty good. Rich, though. Here, try a little." Amy spooned up some and offered it to him. He regarded the concoction a tad suspiciously, but looking game nevertheless, closed his lips around the bite. He nodded agreeably as it melted on his tongue. "You're right," he said, his eyes sparkling with a mixture of pleasure and surprise. "It *is* good."

Amy smiled with the pride of a Charleston native showing off her city, then asked as the two of them sat down at the small round breakfast table, "So how'd you know to go there?"

Nick's knees bumped hers as he tried rather unsuccessfully to get his large frame settled comfortably at the cozy table. "I followed my nose. I figured anything that smelled that good had to taste pretty darn good, too.''

And it did, Amy thought as she dipped a piece of tender pork into her favorite Sticky's condiment, the mustard-based barbecue sauce.

Nick added the ''Hot'' barbecue sauce to his. He inclined his head at the cardboard table and corkboard she'd set up in a corner of the living room. ''What are you doing over there?'' he asked.

Briefly, Amy explained to Nick about finding her long-lost great-aunt Eleanor and the nature of the job. ''Anyway, when I was over at my aunt Winnifred's this afternoon, I took pictures of the carriage house with my digital camera.''

''How long do you have to complete the job?'' Nick asked.

Amy forked up some potato salad. ''She wants it done as soon as possible—in two or three days.''

''Wow.''

''Yeah, I know.''

''That's a lot of pressure.''

Amy regarded Nick confidently. ''I think it'll be fine if I can get her to approve the overall design tomorrow morning.''

Nick took a long thirsty drink of his iced tea. ''What are you going to do about furniture?''

That, Amy thought, as she took a bite of cinnamon apple, was a lot easier. She looked at Nick, noting he was as famished as she was. ''The carriage house is filled with antiques. I took photos of those, too. And that'll help me decide what pieces we're going to use when we redecorate.''

"I'm surprised she doesn't want to start from scratch and buy everything she needs, rather than re-cycle what she already has," Nick said as he ladled more of everything onto his plate. At Amy's look, he shrugged affably. "People of her stature usually do."

"Actually she did want to do that," Amy said, sur-prised and pleased by Nick's intuitive understanding of her business. "I'm the one who vetoed it."

"Why? Wouldn't there be more commission for you if she did buy all new?" he asked casually as he finished the rest of his frogmore stew and dirty rice. "Assuming she's paying you for the work and it's not gratis because she's family."

Amy ate a bite of the tangy coleslaw. "Aunt Win-nifred is paying me—although I tried to get her to accept it as a gift. But she would have none of it."

"Good for her." Nick's eyes met and held Amy's. "People shouldn't take advantage of family."

Amy agreed about that. Family was important, which was why she wanted one of her own so badly.

"So back to what you plan to do for the carriage house," Nick prodded. Finished with their meal, they rose and carried their plates to the sink.

"Basically, what I do for everyone else," Amy said as she rinsed the dishes and loaded the dish-washer, while Nick put the leftover food in the re-frigerator. "I go in, look at what they have, assess what they want and what they need to make that happen.''

Nick shut the refrigerator door and came back to stand beside her. ''You make it sound easy.''

Amy wiped down the table, while he took the plastic bag out of the kitchen garbage container, tied it shut and replaced it with another. Amazed at how easily and effortlessly they were able to work together, Amy smiled at Nick as they walked onto the screened-in back porch and out into the yard. Almost wishing it had taken them longer to get their dinner mess cleaned up—she was enjoying Nick so much she didn't want their time together to end, didn't want to have to go back to work that evening at all—Amy said, ''Redecorating is easy—for me, anyway.''

Nick tossed the day's garbage into the pail and closed the lid, then followed her over to the clothesline. Wordlessly he began helping her collect the now dry linen from the clothesline. ''What's the most common problem you find when you begin a job?''

Amy tossed the clothespins into the wicker basket, one after another. ''Usually people want to throw out too much. Sometimes literally everything.'' She shook her head, marveling at the waste. ''It's almost never necessary.''

As Nick edged closer to her, the tantalizing sandalwood of his aftershave mingled with the clean fragrance of soap and the masculine scent of sweat. Amy's pulse picked up at the unmistakable spark of interest in his eyes, the kind that said he wanted to take her into his arms and kiss her. He continued to hold her gaze. "So in other words, you convince them to appreciate what they have first and then build on that?"

"Right." Amy raked her teeth across her lower lip. "That's what redecorating is all about." She pulled one end of the flat sheet off the line—Nick picked up the other. They folded it in half and then quarters, then walked toward each other, their hands brushing as Nick gave her his end of the sun-dried linen. Struggling against the renewed shimmer of awareness drifting through her, Amy folded the linen into a square and dropped it into the basket on top of the pins, before turning—with Nick—to retrieve the contoured bottom sheet.

Because he looked genuinely interested, she continued explaining how she decorated houses as they folded the trickier elastic-edged sheet. "Sometimes it means taking things from one room and putting them in another. Sometimes it's just poor arrangement of existing pieces or lack of accessorizing what is already there that's the problem. Whatever," Amy shrugged as their hands brushed once again, and Nick took over the final folding of the sheet. "I go in, add a few things and give it a pulled-together look."

Nick dropped the second sheet on top of the first. "I'm guessing business is brisk?"

"Very." Flushing self-consciously, Amy wiggled her bare toes in the grass and admitted, "I actually have a waiting list these days."

Nick looked impressed. "Thought about franchising?" he asked as they each plucked a pillowcase off the line.

Now he sounded like a businessman, like her executive-father or always-looking-for-a-way-to-expand brother, Mitch. Amy picked up the laundry basket and balanced it on her hip. "No." And she wouldn't, either.

Wordlessly Nick took the basket from her and gallantly carried it into the house. "Getting your own TV show, then?" he asked as he led the way to the bedroom, where the stripped double bed waited. He reached over to turn on the bedside lamp, bathing the dusky room with soft light. "Makeovers are tremendously popular with the surge in home-and-garden cable networks."

Amy moved to one side of the bed, Nick the other. "My mother is the TV host in the family, not me," Amy declared.

"A shame." Nick helped her put the sheets on the bed. "You're very photogenic and you have the kind of easygoing personality viewers love."

"I'm still not interested." Amy picked up the quilt, thinking how awfully intimate the bedroom suddenly seemed.

"Any particular reason why not?" Nick asked as they smoothed that, too.

Amy stiffened and tucked a strand of hair behind her ear. "I've seen the way networks treat TV hosts they perceive to be over-the-hill."

"You're talking about your mother's firing from *Rise and Shine, America!*'s" Nick guessed as he sat down on the edge of the bed.

Amy nodded, finding to her surprise that it wasn't just her mother who needed soothing—she needed to talk about it, too. "The network executives were brutal to her. They didn't give her or her cohost a chance to turn the show around. They just came in and replaced her and her colleague with much younger cohosts, and *then* did a complete rehaul of the show." Amy's only satisfaction came from the fact that *Rise and Shine* ratings were continuing to fall. Viewers hated the way the network had treated her mother and her cohost, and were showing their displeasure by turning off the once-beloved morning program in droves.

Nick took Amy's hand and pulled her down to sit beside him. "How's your mom doing?"

Comforted by the compassion and understanding in Nick's eyes, Amy plucked at the fabric of her long, slim-fitting skirt. "It's hard to say. My mother has always been the kind of woman who keeps her emotions under wraps." Unlike Amy, who was well-known for wearing her heart on her sleeve. Even during her parents' separation and divorce, Amy had never really known how her mom was feeling. Deep down, had her mom really wanted the divorce? Amy wondered. Had her dad? Amy had never believed so in her heart. But in the end, Amy's feelings hadn't mattered—her parents had divorced, anyway, and never looked back, or so they both said. Amy still felt her parents belonged together. And would be together, if not for their pride and their certainty that they couldn't fix things enough to be together again.

A small whimper that swiftly crescendoed into an outraged wail sounded from the other room.

"Sounds like Dex is waking up," Nick said as he rolled to his feet.

"He's got to be hungry now," Amy added as she and Nick headed for the nursery. It took only a few seconds to traverse the distance. Nevertheless, by the time they got there, Dexter was wailing at the top of his lungs, his face was red as a beet, and the sheets beneath him were damp and soiled.

"Oh, poor sweetie," Amy murmured, scooping him up gently and holding his flailing body in her arms. "You miss your mommy, don't you? Well, not to worry." She smoothed Dexter's soft hair. "She'll be back soon. Meantime, it's just me and your uncle Nick. But we're going to take very good care of you, I promise."

"Want me to heat the bottle?" Nick asked.

Amy nodded, glad they could work as such a team. "I'll handle the diaper change."

Minutes later Amy was settled in the rocking chair, Dexter cuddled in her arms. Nick, knowing what might have to happen for a successful feeding to occur, discreetly left the living room.

Once again Dexter wasn't happy nursing from a bottle without the softness of a woman's skin against his cheek so Amy unbuttoned her blouse and situated the baby so his face was pressed against the soft skin of the upper part of her breasts.

As Amy had hoped, Dexter calmed immediately. "Okay, little fella," she said, feeling her heart swell with love as she looked into his little face. "This is as close to nursing as we're going to get. So we're both just going to have to deal with it."

His blue eyes widening as if he understood—and agreed—with every word Amy said, Dexter promptly settled down and began to gulp the contents of his bottle in earnest. And that was when the doorbell rang.

Nick strode out of the nursery, where he was busy putting clean sheets on the crib. "You expecting anybody?" he asked as he headed for the door.

"No," Amy said, blushing at having been caught with her bra visible again. She wished she'd thought to get a receiving blanket to throw over her shoulder and provide her with more cover. She wished her lingerie was more modest. But it was lacy and transparent, and damn it, Nick had noticed. She could tell by the sudden darkening of his eyes. She swallowed around the knot of emotion in her throat. "You?"

Nick shook his head. And still looking perplexed, he opened the door.

To Amy's chagrin, on the other side of the threshold was the one person Amy had hoped not to see.

# Chapter Five

"Mom," Amy said.

"Hello, honey." Grace smiled and walked into the cottage with the same poise she'd exhibited whenever she'd crossed the television soundstage. She looked at Nick impersonally, then turned back to Amy, her soft blue eyes vibrating with maternal concern. "Your aunt Winnifred told me you would be here."

Amy did her best not to show any emotion as Nick walked back into the nursery and emerged with a soft blue baby blanket in his hands. "I wanted to see if there was anything I could do," Grace continued with typical Deveraux self-assurance.

*Horse feathers,* Amy thought. *You wanted to check up on me and see if I was going to be safe staying here with Nick.*

Resenting that her mother did not cut her the same slack she did her brothers, Amy said firmly, "Everything is under control, Mom." *Though he has had many opportunities, Nick hasn't made so much as a single pass at me.*

Not that she wanted him to do anything of the sort, Amy hastily reassured herself. No, she was content to have Nick help her baby-sit Dexter and nothing else.

Grace looked at the open lapels of Amy's blouse and then back at Nick, who, as it happened, looked pretty domestic himself, with that baby blanket in his hands. "Are you sure?" Grace asked with a sweetness that did nothing to mask the depth of her concern.

Nick handed the baby blanket to Amy, so she could cover the nursing infant, as well as her breast. He shot Amy a reassuring glance, then closed the distance between himself and Amy's mother, and held out his hand. "Nick Everton," he introduced himself gamely. "Lola's brother and Dexter's uncle."

Recognition flashed in Grace's eyes as they briefly shook hands. "Not *the* Nick Everton," Grace said in surprise.

"If you're referring to the syndicated television producer, that's me," Nick said.

Grace's attention now focused solely on Nick. "I admire the work you've done," Grace told him seriously, all career woman once again. "Your informational programming is the best."

"Thanks." Nick accepted the compliment with sincerity.

Thinking about what Nick planned to propose to her mother, it was all Amy could do not to groan. The last thing she wanted was to be put in a position where she was competing with her superstar mother for anyone's time and attention—especially Nick Everton's. But if Nick had his way, that was exactly what would happen. And Nick and Amy's babysitting teamwork could easily become a thing of the past, as he moved on to accomplish his career objectives, which included signing one of the hottest daytime news and entertainment figures for a syndicated TV show with his production company.

"And I'm sorry to hear about your sister's husband," Grace continued compassionately, completely oblivious to what Nick had planned for her, while Amy—who noticed that Dexter had completely finished his bottle and was now sucking on air—took the bottle away from him, did up her blouse and stood. "Is he going to be all right?" Grace asked.

"I don't know. We certainly hope so," Nick said as Amy looped the baby blanket over Nick's shoulder and handed Dexter to Nick. He positioned Dexter against his chest—a little less awkwardly this time— and glanced at the clock above the mantel. "They're probably still doing surgery on Chuck as we speak," he told Grace.

Grace nodded soberly, then smiled down at Dexter and gently touched his soft cheek. She picked up the edge of the little blanket and dabbed at a milk bubble on the corner of Dexter's mouth. Dexter kicked and cooed contentedly. "Well, we're all hoping and praying for the best possible outcome."

"Thanks." Nick looked at Grace and Amy. There was no denying the tension vibrating between the two. No fool—he knew when to make himself and the baby scarce—Nick cleared his throat. "I think I'll just walk outside with Dexter and check the mailbox, give you two some time to talk alone," he said.

Grace sent Nick a dazzling smile. "I'd appreciate that," Grace dropped her handbag on the sofa.

*I wouldn't,* Amy thought vehemently.

"I really am sorry to hear about Lola's husband," Grace said the moment Nick had gone through the door.

"So am I." Amy was aware that her mother didn't really approve of this baby-sitting business, just as she hadn't approved of Amy's being a volunteer labor coach at Charleston Hospital. Her mother wanted her to spend her spare time dating and looking for someone suitable to settle down with. Absently Amy wondered if Nick, with all his career success, would qualify in Grace's mind.

Amy turned her glance to Chuck's photo on the mantel. Lola's husband looked so young and handsome in his uniform. Amy had never met him, but she knew he was dedicated to his career. "I guess that's part of being in the military, though. You have to accept the dangers and realize you might be injured at some point."

Grace nodded. "Even so, it must be very upsetting for his wife."

"It was—is," Amy said.

"And I understand how difficult it must have been for Lola to leave her baby to go overseas to be with her husband,'' Grace continued sternly ''But is it really necessary for you to become so involved here? After all, the baby's uncle is here.''

Amy wondered what it was going to take to make her family realize that she was an adult now, fully capable of running her life without constant commentary and interference. ''Nick and I are both godparents,'' she said tightly, tired of being treated like a wayward teenager in need of schooling, instead of a twenty-eight-year-old woman who had started a business completely on her own and made it flourish. ''Lola wanted us both here. And Nick needs the help. Dexter's used to being breast-fed and…well, enough said.''

Grace regarded her daughter steadily, no doubt recalling Amy's open blouse and the baby cuddled against her breast. Turning as pink as her elegant summer dress Grace said evenly, ''It's not practical, Amy.''

Amy knew what her mother was getting at, even if she hadn't come right out and said it yet. Grace thought Amy wasn't mature enough to handle staying in such confined quarters with a handsome single man like Nick Everton without succumbing to temptation and ending up in bed with him. ''Not practical or not suitable?'' As far as Amy was concerned, there was a difference. A big one.

Grace looked annoyed. ''You know what I mean, Amy.''

Amy shrugged. ''No one's going to gossip about

our arrangement, Mom, if that's what you're getting at. Heck, the cottage is so far out in the country that no one's even going to know I'm out here alone with Nick and the baby, except members of my own family. And I presume I can trust all of you to protect my reputation, can't I?'' Trusting them all to mind their own business, however, was something else again, Amy knew. As far as everyone in her family was concerned, she was the baby and in need of chaperoning and protection—period.

Grace frowned. ''I don't care what people say. You know that.''

That was true, Amy thought. Her mother didn't listen to, read or repeat gossip.

''I care what you feel.'' Grace closed the distance between them, her arms outstretched. ''That's what worries me.''

The tender look on her mother's face had Amy immediately on edge. ''What do you mean?'' she asked warily as she perched on the arm of the sofa. She could handle her mother's pique a lot better than she could handle her worry.

Grace sat down beside Amy and took her hand. ''We both know how deeply romantic you are at heart. A situation like this...'' Grace sighed and forged on with difficulty, ''Amy, crisis brings people together in ways they would not ordinarily be together.''

Immediately, Amy had an image of herself and Nick wrapped in each other's arms. Not in crisis, but in joy. That it was prompted only by what her mother subtly but unmistakably implied and not in the least bit likely to happen, made the unconscionably sexy image even more disturbing. Flushing self-consciously, Amy turned to her mother and continued, "Let me guess where we're going here. You think I'll get involved with Nick if we're both under the same roof for any time at all." Amy regarded her mother as if the possibility hadn't occurred to her at all, when deep inside she knew, for reasons she didn't really understand, that it already had.

Grace shrugged and said gently, "You're human, Amy. Maybe even a little lonely for male companionship. And you and Nick are both young and attractive. Being here together in such a small space for days on end will create an aura of intimacy and closeness, a feeling that you are both in this together as you take care of Dexter for Lola and Chuck. Don't you see how one thing might naturally lead to another? A kiss, a look, another kiss? I just don't want to see you hurt again."

Amy turned away as she recalled how foolish she had been once, how she had repeatedly and steadfastly ignored her mother's advice not to get so involved with Kirk so quickly.

But Kirk had been all wrong for her.

Was Nick?

Amy folded her arms in front of her. "I won't be hurt," she stated stubbornly, giving her mother a look that told her to back off.

"That's what you thought about—"

"And you were right about Kirk and I was wrong," Amy interrupted, bounding to her feet. She began to pace the small room, her long skirt clinging to her legs, her bare feet moving soundlessly on the wood floor and wool area rug. "But that was then and this is now. And Nick and I are not going to get involved."

"Sure about that?" Grace queried, her concern about the situation unabated. "Because I already see you wearing your emotions on your sleeve. And I know how much you adored playing house as a kid."

That was true, Amy thought, but playing house had been nothing like this.

The door opened. Amy looked up with relief as Nick came in, carrying Dexter in one arm, a stack of mail in the other. "Everything okay in here?" he asked genially.

Amy could tell by the look in Nick's eyes that he knew everything wasn't okay, which was why he had come in. "Everything's fine," Amy said. She took Dexter from Nick and put the infant on her shoulder to burp him. "In fact," Amy continued pleasantly, "my mom was just about to leave."

Grace got the hint and reached for her handbag. "Just so you know, Amy, I'm available day or night, any time you need me. All you have to do is call."

"Thanks, Mom," Amy said quietly. Although she and her mother rarely saw eye to eye on anything, she did love Grace and wanted her approval. Very much. She just never really seemed to be able to get it, not the way her brothers did. And that frustrated her immensely. She didn't want to be regarded as the child of Grace's who had no common sense, but knew that was exactly how her mom saw her most of the time.

"I'll walk you out to your car," Nick told her mother.

"Thank you," Grace said.

Amy watched them go. To her dismay, the two of them did not immediately bid each other adieu. Instead, Nick lingered beside Grace's car, talking animatedly, smiling often, all ruggedly handsome male. By the time he did come in, she had just about given up on him ever doing so. "That certainly took a long time," she noted, doing her best to mask her real feelings.

Nick smiled. "Your mom is very charming."

Amy had heard that often over the years. Usually the expression of such sentiments made her proud and happy. Tonight she felt wary and on edge. Deciding to cut straight to the chase, she looked Nick in the eye and asked, "Did she say anything to you?"

Nick's mouth curved ruefully. He thrust his hands in his pockets and sauntered closer. Dropping to his haunches beside her and Dexter on the sofa, he reached over to smooth the curling tufts of pale hair on Dexter's head. "Besides warning me not to break your heart, you mean?"

Amy winced at the image the words presented. She

turned toward Nick, her thigh brushing the length of his. "Did she really say that?" Amy studied his face.

Abruptly, worry crept into Nick's eyes. "Not in so many words, but yeah, that was the gist of it. She seems to think you're very fragile." He gave her a steady look that set her pulse to pounding, then tucked an errant strand of hair behind her ear. "Are you?"

Amy tingled all over at the soft timbre of his tone and touch. Unless she got a hold of herself, and soon, who knew what might happen? "I'm a Deveraux," she announced breezily. "I'm as tough as they come."

"Good. Glad to hear it." Nick shifted Dexter from Amy's lap to his, then settled against Amy companionably, stretching his long legs out in front of him. "So, what are your plans for the evening?" He asked, his shoulder nudging hers.

*Besides trying like heck not to fantasize about where this might lead when the two of us are living together in this cozy little country cottage, playing mommy and daddy to one of the most adorable little babies on earth?* Amy wondered. Doing her best to keep a level head, Amy moved gracefully to her feet. She propped her hands on her hips. She could feel the blood rushing to her cheeks as she struggled to get a handle on her soaring emotions. This was not going to be a romantic evening, she warned herself sternly. In truth, it was going to be anything but. "I want to give Dexter a bath and put him in some pajamas. And I think I'm going to need your help with that.''

''Okay.'' Nick smiled and stood, too, Dexter still cradled lovingly—and happily—in his arms.

Trying hard not to think how it would feel to be held so lovingly against that broad chest, Amy continued soberly, ''And then I've got to work.''

Nick sighed, looking about as thrilled as she was. ''Me, too.''

NICK HADN'T BEEN kidding, Amy found out later. As soon as Dexter was asleep again, Nick hauled out his laptop computer and cell phone. He carried both to the screened-in porch, turned on the overhead lights and got busy. While she sat inside and prepared a computer-generated proposal for her aunt, he sat outside and talked business and typed out one memo after another.

Finally, around 11:00 p.m., they were both finished, and Dexter woke up again.

Amy glanced at her watch. ''Every four hours, like clockwork.''

''I don't suppose Lola mentioned to you if he sleeps through the night yet, did she?'' Nick asked hopefully, as he changed a diaper that stunk to high heaven.

Amy took it from him, wrapped it in a plastic bag and dropped it into the airtight pail on the floor with the deodorizer lid. Then she stepped into the bathroom across the hall to wash her hands. ''He doesn't," she finally answered from the bathroom. "Dexter's nighttime bottle is at 3:00 a.m." She dried her hands and went back into the nursery.

Nick was clumsily trying to get the legs of Dexter's sleeper snapped, Unfortunately the side he had already done was one off at the ankle, which meant, Amy knew as she stepped in to assist, that it all had to be redone.

"At 3:00 a.m.," Nick repeated.

Amy groaned, just thinking about it.

Nick shot her a look that would have melted her knees to mush under other circumstances. A knowing smile spread from his mouth to his eyes as he picked up the now-fully-dressed Dexter up and handed him to Amy, then walked across the hall to wash his hands, too. "You're one of those people who needs a lot of sleep, aren't you."

Amy debated pleading the Fifth as Nick dried his hands and took physical charge of his nephew once again. Together, they headed companionably for the kitchen. "Define a lot." Aware Nick looked even sexier than he had earlier in the day, she went to the refrigerator to retrieve another bottle of Lola's breast milk.

Nick shrugged as she put the bottle in the microwave and turned it on. "Six or seven hours."

Amy made a face. "Actually, I like to have around eight if I can get it." His gray eyes lit up merrily. "How much do you usually get?" Amy asked as she shelved the mental image of the two of them running into each other in their nightclothes in the middle of the night.

Nick moved closer, looking annoyingly at ease. "Four or five."

Determined not to show how much his nearness was affecting her, Amy lifted an insouciant brow. "That's all?"

Nick shrugged, his broad shoulders straining against the soft knit fabric of his polo shirt. "That's all I need," he said as Amy shook the warmed bottle and tested the milk on her wrist. "And since that's the case," Nick continued, "I'll get up with Dexter in the middle of the night and change his diaper and give him his bottle."

Amy walked out onto the porch, which was now lit only by twin sconces on the wall, and sat on the swing. The late-spring evening was sensuously warm, the air softly scented with flowers. As an experiment, she put Dexter against her breasts, without unbuttoning her blouse and offered him the bottle. Once again, he refused to take it, as long as his face was resting against her shirt. "I thought you weren't comfortable doing that," Amy said as she unbuttoned her blouse, and settled Dexter's cheek against her breast. Almost immediately, he began to take big, thirsty gulps of his mother's milk.

Nick glanced at the two of them. "He seems to have settled down a little," Nick said, as he stretched his arm companionably along the back of the swing. With his free hand, he captured one of Dexter's fists

and lifted it to his mouth for a kiss. "Besides, you'll
be right here in the next room if I do run into any
problem." Tenderly, Nick held on to Dexter's chubby
little fist. "And I can try feeding him without a shirt,
too."

Amy contemplated that possibility. If Nick's chest
was as sexy as the rest of him, she was going to have
a lot more fuel for her romantic fantasies than she
needed. Not that she planned to act on any of those
fantasies, she reminded herself sternly. Nick and she
were only here to baby-sit.

She cleared her throat, noting that Dexter had already drained the bottle in record time and was once
again sucking on air. She took the bottle from him
and shifted him over to Nick for burping.

"You're going to sleep on the sofa?" Hastily, Amy
buttoned her blouse.

Nick shrugged as he turned Dexter onto his tummy
and laid the infant across his lap. Gently, Nick rubbed
Dexter's back from shoulders to spine. "Unless you
want to take the sofa and give me the bed." Still
holding firmly to the infant on his lap, Nick turned to
look at Amy, his gaze roving her hair, cheeks, nose
and lips before returning to her eyes. His lips curved
in a warm smile as he shook his head and said, "But
I doubt I could live with that."

"Why not?" Amy asked, mesmerized by his closeness, as well as by the look in his eyes.

Nick shrugged again. "The gentleman in me, I
guess. It wouldn't be right for me to take the bed if

you had the sofa.'' His eyes sparkled with teasing lights. ''Of course we could always share the bed,'' he said, knowing without asking what the answer to that would be.

Amy couldn't help but smile, too—maybe because she knew he wasn't the least bit serious about the proposition. ''Ha, ha. Very funny.''

''I thought so.'' Nick grinned, all male, as the silence stretched between them, more intimate and fun-filled than ever. He winked at her. ''Then, the sofa it is.''

TAKING THE SOFA had seemed the right thing to do—until Nick actually tried to fit on the cottage-size furniture. There was no way he could lie down and stretch his legs out, not without his legs going up and over the raised arm of the sofa and dangling in the air from the knee down. If he lay on his side and bent his legs at the knees so his feet were on the sofa, his knees were way off the edge.

He could always drag his blanket down to the floor and lie down in front of the fireplace. Then he'd have as much room to stretch out as he wanted. But he would also be sleeping on a wool rug on a wood floor. And a night trying to get comfortable on solid-oak planking didn't appeal to him, either.

Sighing, Nick got up, moved the coffee table next to the wall out of harm's way and then carried the ottoman over to the sofa. He pulled the upholstered footrest flush against the sofa, aligning it where he thought his knees would land, then lay back down again, rolled onto his side and did his best to curl up on the two pieces of juxtaposed furniture. It wasn't a perfect solution, but it still beat the floor.

And it was a place to sleep. He wasn't in an unfamiliar campground or in the back of a beat-up old van. He had a roof over his head, plenty of food in his stomach and no noisy neighbors. So why couldn't he drift off? Nick wondered torturously long moments later. Why did he see Amy Deveraux's face every time he closed his eyes? Nick supposed it was her proximity bothering him, the sweet innocence in her gaze, the gentleness of her manner and the loving way she cared for Dexter, even as she challenged Nick to be a better, more giving man than he actually was. He hadn't slept under the same roof with a woman since his life had been turned upside down years ago. Instead, he had let his work fill up the numbing emptiness of his life and made sure that when he was with a woman, they both knew it was a pleasurable but strictly physical thing that did not include sleeping over or emotional intimacy. It had been either that or live out his life alone and give up altogether. And for reasons Nick still couldn't understand, he had not been able to do that.

He'd had to go on. Hour by hour. Day by day. Until his life seemed almost normal again. Normal, but so empty that no amount of money or professional success could fill the void. Because Nick knew what Amy Deveraux didn't, that he had failed when it had mattered most, he was never—ever—going to put himself or anyone else in that position again.

He would live up to his obligations and care for his sister, his nephew. But he wasn't going to get involved or married or have a family. He wasn't going to let down those closest to him ever again.

As it was, he had enough guilt and regret in him to last a lifetime. No way was he asking for more. Not even if Amy Deveraux was the prettiest, sexiest, sweetest woman he had met in a very long time. No matter how attracted he was to her or wished things were otherwise. He had promised Amy's mother and his sister, Lola, both of whom had immediately sensed the chemistry simmering between him and Amy, that he would not do anything to hurt Amy or destroy her already fragile heart. And that was a promise he meant to keep.

# Chapter Six

Amy awoke to the sound of Dexter stirring. That was followed by a loud thud and a lot of heartfelt swearing. Aware it sounded as if both males needed help, Amy flung the covers away from her and rolled out of bed, grabbing her long white eyelet-lace robe as she went. Two steps later she was at the bedroom door, then out in the living room. Moonlight streamed in through the windows. And Nick was just getting up...from the floor? Her heart pounding at the sight of him in nothing but a pair of low-slung silk pajama pants, Amy rushed over to give Nick a hand. He grimaced as she helped him to his feet, while in the nursery, Dexter had quieted once again. "What happened?" Amy asked Nick breathlessly, trying not to sound as alarmed as she felt.

"I tried to get up to go and get Dexter and tripped on the ottoman," Nick muttered as he reached for a light switch and turned it on.

Amy frowned as she regarded the upholstered footstool, now in the center of the room. She knew it hadn't been there earlier. She would never have left it there in the middle of the room where someone could get hurt. "What's that doing there?" she asked, glancing back at Nick and doing her best to tear her eyes from the soft whorls of hair arrowing downward on his muscled chest.

Nick shrugged, his powerful shoulders flexing as he bent and rubbed his shin. "Long story," he said in the same low tone as he took in her long white nightgown with the snug bodice and spaghetti straps. One he apparently didn't want to go into, Amy thought with chagrin. Nick placed a reassuring hand on her arm, his warm palm sending a tingle of awareness shimmering straight to Amy's toes. "You can go back to bed." Nick seemed irritated to be found in less-than-perfect form.

"I'm awake now," Amy said as she pulled on her robe over her nightgown and fastened the two pearl buttons at her breast. Down the hall, she could hear Dexter stirring, a lot less patiently now, in the nursery. "I might as well give you a hand," she said as Dexter let out a loud angry wail. "You get the bottle, I'll go get Dexter."

Talking to the baby softly all the while, Amy changed his diaper, hoping a dry bottom would relieve his distress. Instead, it only seemed to make him feel worse. He wailed pitifully at first, then with increasing volume. "There now," Amy said as she snapped the legs of his terry-cloth sleeper. "Nick is coming," she soothed—to no avail.

Dexter kicked his legs out straight, then drew them up to his chest and, fists clenched tight, waved his arms around his head.

Looking concerned by Dexter's crying, Nick strode back with the bottle. "Okay, buddy," he said. "Here it is."

"Did you test it?" Amy asked, as she picked Dexter up again and settled into the rocking chair in the living room.

Nick nodded. "Yes. But it probably wouldn't hurt to do it again." Still looking sexy as all get-out, with his hair all tousled and his handsome face rimmed with stubble, Nick pushed back the sleeve of Amy's robe and sprinkled a little formula on Amy's arm. "Feel good to you?" he asked.

Aware all over again of what a good team they made, Amy nodded. "It feels perfect, Nick."

She put the bottle to Dexter's lips. He spit it out and waved his arms harder, squalling all the while. Figuring maybe Dexter just needed to feel the warmth of her bare skin again, Amy opened her robe and settled Dexter's head just above the neckline of her nightgown. Unfortunately this time the touch of Amy's skin did nothing to soothe him. Dexter only squirmed and cried harder. For the next five minutes, first Amy—and then Nick—tried everything they could think of to soothe the increasingly upset infant.

To no avail. Finally Amy headed for the phone. "I'm calling my brother, Gabe," she said.

Nick followed Amy, a crying Dexter in his arms. "What's he going to do?"

"Gabe's a doctor. He'll let us know if Dexter is all right."

"WHAT'S THE PROBLEM?" Amy asked her brother as soon as he had finished examining Dexter from head to toe. "What's making him so fussy?"

Gabe Deveraux unhooked the stethoscope from around his neck and put it back in his medical bag. Although a newlywed, he hadn't complained when Amy had asked him to get out of bed and come over, to take a look at the ailing infant. "Dexter has a lot of excess air in his tummy that's causing him some discomfort. That's probably why he's flailing around so much and refusing a bottle. He swallows even more air when he cries, which only adds to the problem."

"So how do we fix this?" Amy asked worriedly as she refastened the snaps of Dexter's sleeper yet again. Caring for a healthy baby was responsibility enough; watching over an ailing child was an even more daunting prospect. And judging by the deeply concerned look on Nick's face, he was feeling the same way.

Gabe smiled at Amy reassuringly, looking every inch the excellent physician he was. "First, we'll give Dexter some drops to absorb the excess air and make him stop hurting.'' Gabe took a small bottle of medicine out of his bag. He filled the dropper to the appropriate mark and then deftly inserted the medicine into Dexter's mouth. Dexter stopped crying long enough to taste the cherry-flavored serum, then took a big breath and started crying again. Gabe picked up Dexter and soothed him gently with soft words and several pats on the back, then handed Dexter to Nick.

''What can we do to prevent this from happening again?'' Nick asked as he walked Dexter back and forth, soothing him with gentle strokes of his hand, until the infant's cries started to subside.

''For starters,'' Gabe replied, ''his feedings should take twenty minutes.''

''He's been doing them in five or ten,'' Amy said.

Gabe frowned in concern. ''If he's that hungry, he may not be getting enough calories. Did Lola say anything about her pediatrician starting Dexter on solid food yet, to supplement his diet?''

Amy nodded. ''Actually she was going to start Dexter on rice cereal yesterday, but she didn't have time to do it before she left for Germany.'' There was an unopened box of baby cereal in the cupboard. Amy had seen it when she'd been putting groceries away earlier.

''Well, normally I'd say wait until Lola returned, but under the circumstances, maybe you two should go ahead and try it. Give Dexter a spoonful or two of cereal mixed with formula or breast milk tomorrow morning before he takes his bottle, and see if that helps fill him up. If he tolerates it well, you can give him a very small amount two or three times a day. Also, make sure you stop and burp him several times during the bottle feeding. That might help, too. And keep a bottle of these drops on hand—they're available over the counter at the pharmacy.''

"Okay. We'll do that tomorrow," Amy said.

"And also check the nipples on the bottles—make sure they aren't allowing the milk to come out too fast. If they are, buy some new ones with smaller holes."

Nick and Amy nodded. "Thanks for helping us out here," Nick told Amy's older brother gratefully as Dexter, completely exhausted, finally wound down enough to stop crying and curled against Nick's chest.

AMY SMILED at the tender picture Nick and his nephew made. Gabe, however, frowned and took Amy by the arm, saying to Nick, "Amy and I'll be right back." Giving her no chance to protest, Gabe steered Amy into the bedroom. He shut the door behind him and indicated she should sit down on the rumpled covers of the double bed. "You want to explain to me what's going on here?" he said in his sternest big-brother tone.

"No, actually, I don't." Ignoring the fact that she was still in her nightgown and matching robe, Amy stood and started to brush by Gabe.

Gabe moved to block her way. "Amy," he warned sternly, "you're my little sister."

"Tell me something I don't know," she retorted dryly, sensing a lecture coming on.

"And you're all heart," Gabe continued. "But this is not a good situation for you to be in."

Amy fought a self-conscious blush and folded her arms. "And why is that?" she asked defiantly. Her mother had covered much the same ground earlier.

"Because the situation is way too cozy for you and Nick Everton, that's why. I don't have any problem with you helping care for your friend Lola's baby, or helping Nick out, but sleeping under the same roof and being around each other at all hours of the day and night is just not smart!"

Given the unorthodox way Gabe and his wife, Maggie, had gotten together, Amy did not think he had room to talk. She shook her head. "We're not together all the time."

"Enough to cause a problem," Gabe argued. "Which is why I think you need to come up with a less-intimate living arrangement."

Amy drew a deep breath and propped her hands on her hips. It was bad enough her mother had stopped by to deliver this message, but to get it from Gabe—the brother she was closest to—was more than she could take. "Are you finished?" she asked impatiently.

Gabe exhaled every bit as loudly as she had inhaled. He looked unhappy that he hadn't made her see reason. "I guess I am," he said in a low frustrated tone, frowning more fiercely.

Amy led the way out of the bedroom and waited for him to collect his medical bag. ''I'll walk you to your car,'' she said quietly, noting that Nick, who looked like a worried parent, had settled into the rocking chair with a drowsy Dexter cuddled against his bare chest. She paused to slip on her sandals before heading out the door. ''And, Gabe…thanks for coming by.''

''No problem,'' Gabe reached over to give her a hug goodbye as they reached his car. ''You know I love you and would do anything for you.''

Amy smiled as she returned the embrace. ''I love you, too,'' she said. Now, Amy thought, drawing an exasperated breath, if she could only get him and the rest of her family to stop advising her on how to lead her life, she'd be all set.

''OKAY, DEXTER, this is going to be something different this morning. But the writing on the box assures us you are going to just love this rice cereal,'' Amy said as she spooned up a quarter teaspoon of the creamy rice cereal that had been measured and stirred to perfection. ''And the baby pictured on the box eating this stuff looks pretty happy, too.''

His nephew couldn't have cared less, however, Nick noted.

Except, Dexter made a face when it hit his tongue, then immediately pushed it back out again. Amy caught the blob with the edge of his silver baby spoon before it could hit his bib. She raked her teeth across her soft lower lip.

Watching her, Nick couldn't help but think how pretty she looked, even after a night of very little sleep. It was only 7:00 a.m., but she had already showered and changed into a pair of snug-fitting white jeans, sneakers and a turquoise T-shirt, with her company logo written across the front. Her hair had been caught in a bouncy ponytail on the back of her head. Her eyes were bright and lively with the thrill of trying something new. "How about one more time?" she asked Dexter cheerfully as she put the spoon against his lips and tried again.

Looking even more skeptical than he had the first time, Dexter spit out the food again.

Amy sighed and switched places with Nick. As he sat down in front of the infant seat, which had been placed on the kitchen table, she handed the spoon to him. "Maybe you'll have more luck."

Nick doubted it—Amy was the one with the golden touch when it came to parenting—but he was willing to give it a try. "Think I should pretend it's a choo-choo train or airplane?" he said.

Amy folded her arms on the table in front of her and leaned closer, the tantalizing apple-blossom freshness of her hair and skin inundating his senses. "Whatever you think will work."

"All right. Then a choo-choo train it is." Amy chuckled as Nick made a chugging and then a whistling sound. Dexter was so stunned he didn't know what to think. When his cherubic mouth dropped open, Nick slid the cereal in. Dexter let it rest on his tongue, not exactly swallowing it, but not exactly spitting it out, either.

"By George, I think we've got it!" Amy teased as Nick managed to get Dexter to take another eighth of a teaspoon of creamy cereal. She laid her hand on his arm. "I think you have the magic touch."

Nick wished that was so.

One thing was certain. He enjoyed spending time with Amy. To the point where he couldn't really say he minded them sharing space or sleeping under the same roof. And that was a change. Except for his relationship with his sister, he had avoided any kind of emotional intimacy for years now and had expected to keep on doing the same. Being around Amy—and Dexter—and finding it a lot easier than he'd thought had made him begin to rethink that.

The doorbell rang. Amy glanced at the kitchen clock. It was only seven-thirty. She pushed back her chair and stood, her knee brushing his thigh in the process. "Who in the world could that be?" she said, frowning.

She strode across the combination living, kitchen and dining area to the window. "Darn it!"

"Who is it?" Nick asked. Aware Dexter had just about finished the tablespoon they'd prepared for him, Nick wiped his tiny mouth.

"My other brothers!" Amy stormed.

Somehow Nick was not surprised. He'd had the

feeling the Deveraux weren't finished circling the wagons around their beloved only daughter/sister. All that was lacking now was a visit from her father. Amy flung open the door, but did not invite her brothers in. "What are you two doing here?" Nick heard her demand.

Figuring his presence was not only required, but advisable, given the amount of anger in Amy's usually sweet-natured tone, Nick picked Dexter up out of his baby seat and carried him to the door.

"Hey." The one in the beach shorts and loose-fitting shirt inclined his head at Nick and extended his hand. "Chase Deveraux."

"Nick Everton." Nick shifted Dexter to his left arm and shook hands with Chase.

"And I'm Mitch Deveraux," the man next to him in the dark business suit said. "Also Amy's brother."

Nick shook hands with him, too. "Nice to meet you both," he said. Nick moved to step back. "Won't you come in?"

Stubbornly, Amy moved to block her brothers' way. "I really don't think that's necessary," she said, fire in her eyes. "I'm sure Chase needs to get to his magazine office. And Mitch probably needs to be at Deveraux Shipping."

"We've got time to say hello," Chase said with exaggerated pleasantness.

"Well, *we* don't." Amy gently nudged Nick—and Dexter—aside and tried to shut the door in her brothers' faces. Mitch caught it and held it open, then regarded Amy stoically. "Gabe told us you refused to listen to his advice last night."

Amy's eyes turned stormy. "Then he probably also told you that I advised him—a lot more politely than I'm prepared to tell you—to butt out of my business!"

Chase rolled his eyes and shoved a hand through his hair. "Look, we all know how stubborn you can be about admitting you made a bad decision," he said, taking hold of Amy's wrist and tugging her out to stand beside him and Mitch on the front porch. "That you will go to whatever lengths required to make something that shouldn't work, work! But you don't have to stick with this one, Amy, the way you stuck with Kirk. There's still time to back out of it gracefully." He spoke as if underlining every word.

Amy folded her arms stubbornly. "Suppose I don't want to back out of it gracefully or any other way?" she shot back.

Mitch and Chase exchanged glances. "Then you're in deeper than we thought," Mitch said gravely, his concern for his younger sister evident.

"Look, I don't want to interfere in a family argument here," Nick said, glad he was no longer in just his silk pajama pants, but had also showered, shaved and dressed for the day. "But if there is some way I can help..." he offered politely.

"There isn't, since my brothers were just leaving," Amy snapped.

Chase Deveraux, who had obviously given up on

talking sense into his sister, turned to Nick. "Mitch and I stopped by to offer you the use of my beach house," Chase said.

"Or my condominium," Mitch said.

"You could live at either place you want, and Amy could stay here with the baby," Chase suggested bluntly to Nick.

"Which would eliminate some of the trickier aspects of trying to coexist in such a small space," Mitch said.

Giving Nick no chance to respond to their generous offers with the not-so-hidden agenda of keeping Nick and Amy apart as much as possible, Amy shook her head, defiantly nixing both ideas. She propped her hands on her hips and regarded both her brothers stonily. "Nick and I promised Lola we would *both* stay right here and take care of Dexter in her absence. So we're *both* going to do it."

Mitch gave Nick a man-to-man glance. Through talking reason to his sister, as well, he threw himself on Nick's mercy. "You've got to understand why we disapprove of this arrangement," he said plainly.

"Actually—" Nick sighed, looking both Mitch Deveraux and Chase Deveraux in the eye "—I do."

"THANKS FOR NOTHING," Amy grumbled resentfully as soon as her brothers had left.

"What did you want me to say?" Nick asked as he carried a sleepy Dexter back to his crib and gently settled him in for a nap. Exhausted by the morning's activity and excitement, Dexter closed his eyes almost immediately. Satisfied all was well with his nephew at least, Nick steered Amy out of the nursery and into the living room. He knew she was furious with him, and though, for as far back as he could recall, his impulse was usually to walk away from emotional confrontations like this, he knew he couldn't do that here. Not with the two of them still charged with caring for Dexter and living under the same roof.

Amy's turquoise eyes sparkled with hurt. Her lusciously soft lower lip took on a sulky pout. "You could have defended what we were doing here," she corrected him icily, "instead of agreeing with my brothers that the two of us staying here together is risky at best."

Nick sighed, aware he wanted nothing more at that moment than to simply take Amy in his arms and kiss away all her cares. Which was, ironically, precisely what her extended family was so worried about. That the two of them would end up getting physically and emotionally close because of their proximity to each other and the fact they'd been thrown together in a situation not of their choosing. Nick knew if he ever took Amy to bed, it had to be because it felt right to him, not because they were in an us-against-the-world frame of mind.

Nick gripped her shoulders lightly and waited for her to lift her face to his. "Listen to me, Amy," he counseled sternly. "What we're attempting to do here is noble. The way it looks—the two of us running around at all hours of the day and night in such tight quarters—is not. And if you were honest with yourself, you'd admit that.''

She regarded him in stony silence, not about to admit that or anything else.

Nick sighed. Knowing that he had to take another tack and that there was more than he had yet been told behind her family's reaction to her temporary living situation with him, Nick let her go and asked lightly, ''So who's Kirk? And what did he do that still has your brothers so riled?''

Amy threw her hands up and spun around. Her hips moving sexily in the nice-fitting white jeans, she headed for the back porch. She shot Nick a beleaguered glance over her shoulder as she opened the lid of the washing machine. ''It's more like what he *didn't* do,'' she said evenly as she measured a cup of baby laundry detergent and put it in the machine.

''Which was…?'' Nick prodded, watching as she set the dials to hot-water wash and rinse.

Amy sighed loudly. ''Succeed—at anything.''

Nick positioned himself so he could see her face. Folding his arms across his chest, he leaned against the wall beside the machine. Content to take his time finding out what he wanted to know, he let his eyes drift over her hair and face. ''I don't get it.''

Amy turned on the water and waited for the machine to fill. A mixture of regret and resignation turned the corners of her lips down and darkened the irises of her eyes. ''If you must know,'' she replied wearily, "I started dating Kirk in college. My family never approved of him because he wasn't as ambitious and hard-driving as they would've liked."

Nick could imagine how that would have gone over with the hard-driving successful Deveraux family. Her brother Chase had his own magazine, her brother Mitch was second-in-command at Deveraux Shipping, her father ran the company, and her brother Gabe—who was at the moment the motivating force behind the powerful show of familial concern—was a well-respected critical-care doctor. The women in the Deveraux family were no slouches, either. Amy's mother, Grace, was one of the best-known figures in the morning news and entertainment business. And Amy had started her own redecorating business and made it flourish. So she, too, was inherently driven and ambitious.

Nick looked at her curiously. "And that didn't bother you?"

Amy looked into the machine, saw the detergent had dissolved nicely and picked up a hamper of soiled infant clothing. Sorting quickly and methodically as she went, she dropped the clothes item by item into the machine, putting the darks and colored items in a pile to one side. "I thought he just needed to be more self-assured, to be with someone who really believed in him." Amy paused to spray spot remover to a particularly bad stain.

"So I'm guessing you gave Kirk lots of support

and encouragement,'' Nick murmured, knowing how kindhearted a person Amy was.

"That and more," Amy said dryly. Finished with the whites and pastels, she dropped the lid and let the machine continue to fill. "For five long years I gave him every chance in the world. My cheerleading never worked, of course. Kirk was what he was, a sort of carefree, unambitious guy who lived only in the moment and never stayed with any one interest for long."

Nick could see how that must have rankled. "So how did it end?"

Shrugging her slender shoulders, she explained in a low, weary voice, "Kirk got tired of me pushing him to be something he wasn't. And he finally broke up with me two years ago, when I was twenty-six." Not giving Nick a chance to comment, Amy rushed on self-effacingly, "And you know what the really sad part is? Had Kirk not ended it for the two of us when he did," she concluded in bitter resignation, "I might still be hanging in there, trying to somehow make things work."

Which explained, Nick thought, what had her family so concerned. They didn't want her getting involved with or wasting her life on another man who wasn't right for her. He searched her eyes, wishing all the while he could do more to comfort her, like take her in his arms.

"You have a hard time admitting you're wrong about someone?" he asked casually, forcing the unbidden impulse away. *He would not get romantically involved with her. He would not hurt her the way she'd already been hurt.*

"I don't know if it's that so much as it's that I have a hard time giving up on people in general," Amy explained. Wanting Nick to understand, she moved closer and looked deeply into his eyes. "You see, I always think a person can be all they want or hope to be, if they just give it half a try. And I just didn't want to hear my family tell me they had been right about Kirk all along, that he wasn't the guy for me, after all. That we were too different and I never should have gotten involved with him in the first place."

Nick could understand that. He didn't like I-told-you-so's, either. Figuring they could both use another cup of coffee, he took Amy by the hand and led her into the kitchen. He motioned for her to sit down at the table while he went over to the coffeemaker and set about brewing a fresh pot. "What eventually happened to Kirk, do you know?"

At that, Amy looked even more distressed. "He's still in the Charleston area, drifting from job to job, working only when he feels like it. But a lot of time he doesn't work and he doesn't mind that, either."

Nick sat down opposite her at the small round table for two. "I can see why that didn't go over well with your family."

"You're right about that." Amy rubbed the tense muscles in her neck. "The Deveraux have a very strong work ethic. To not be busy and productive all the time is unthinkable. Anyway,'' Amy continued in frustration, dropping her hand and looking Nick straight in the eye, ''I know there are times when I'm unrealistically optimistic in my expectations and should give up, but there's something in me that resists the idea of quitting—anything.'' Her chin took on a stubborn tilt as she waited for his reaction to her bold statement. ''And I don't necessarily think that's a bad thing.''

Nick grinned at Amy's feisty attitude. ''Tenaciousness can be a valuable quality to have in business and in life,'' he agreed readily. On impulse, he reached over and took both her hands in his. ''But none of that has anything to do with what your brothers are concerned about,'' he told her gently. ''They just don't want to see you hurt.''

Amy regarded Nick steadily, her fingers tightening on his as she flashed him a trusting smile. ''You wouldn't hurt me,'' Amy said.

Guilt rushed through Nick at the thought of his response to that statement. Because he *would* end up hurting her if he did what he had been tempted to do since he'd first laid eyes on her and took her in his arms and kissed her the way he wanted to kiss her— deeply and passionately.

''You don't know that,'' Nick countered calmly, hoping—for Amy's sake—to resurrect some of the emotional barriers between them that they had just torn down. ''Because you don't really know me.''

Realizing the coffee had finished brewing, Nick stood.

"I know Lola," Amy countered just as insistently. She got to her feet, too. "And Lola loves you and thinks you're terrific. So that's all the information I need."

Nick had the feeling Amy would not be satisfied until she knew him inside and out, even if she hadn't yet admitted it to herself. "I still don't want to be the cause of grief between you and your family," Nick countered calmly as he took two mugs from the cupboard. Nor did he want to turn Amy's seemingly well-ordered life upside down. And if he got involved with her romantically and had the kind of wild and exciting fling he could easily see them having and then walked away, as was his custom these days, he would hurt her. No question.

Amy studied him through narrowed eyes. "You don't want to upset my family? Or my mother and the business deal you'd like to make with her?" she asked.

Nick paused. Even though it wasn't necessarily going to paint him in a positive light, he wasn't going to lie to her. He regarded her steadily. "I would prefer not to lose the opportunity to work with your mother."

Her pique showing in the pink flush in her cheeks, Amy asked, "To the point you'd ignore your sister's wishes and stay somewhere other than this cottage if that were the only way to appease my family?"

Good question, Nick thought. And one he already knew the answer to. If he had to choose between his family and business obligations, it would be family. And if he had to choose between being close to Amy and doing business with her sought-after mother, he was stunned to find he would choose his friendship with Amy. Which could only mean that he was beginning to get in over his head here. Beginning to want not just friendship with Amy, but something more. And something more could mean trouble for both of them.

"I would hope that wouldn't be necessary," Nick said soberly just as the phone rang.

"But if it was," Amy persisted.

"Then I choose this," Nick said in a low distracted voice as he made a grab for the receiver before it could wake the sleeping baby. To Nick's relief, it was his sister, calling from the military hospital in Germany. Nick listened intently to her report on Chuck, then told her how things were going on the home front. He explained about the house call Gabe had made and the prescribed changes they were making to prevent Dexter from having any more stomachaches. Nick ended the conversation by telling her to take care of her husband, and that they'd talk soon.

Nick hung up the phone and turned to Amy, who was standing next to the kitchen sink, waiting anxiously for an update. "Chuck's surgery was a complete success—he's just been moved out of recovery. He's facing two or three more days in the hospital and several months of physical rehabilitation after that, but the doctors have said he's not going to be paralyzed.''

Amy pressed a hand to her chest and breathed a huge sigh of relief. ''Oh, Nick. That is such good news.''

Nick regarded her happily. ''Yeah, isn't it?''

He and Amy fell silent, smiling at each other, thinking how lucky they were things hadn't gone the other way. As Nick knew they so easily could have. ''So now all we have to worry about,'' Nick concluded pragmatically, his mind already moving ahead to the next problem to be solved, ''is getting your family to realize that I am no threat, romantic or otherwise, to you.''

# Chapter Seven

"Which means what?" Amy said, not sure why his matter-of-fact pronouncement should bother her so much, just knowing it did. Maybe because he was much more able to dismiss and walk away from what she felt happening between them than she was. "You're not planning to kiss me or put the moves on me, are you?"

Nick continued to look at her in a very sexy, very determined way. "No."

Amy's heart accelerated. She hated that he looked so at ease when she was tied up in knots. "What if I kiss you or put the moves on you?" she asked, her mind already filled with the images of the two of them in bed.

Nick regarded her with maddening confidence as his gaze roved over her, taking in her hair, face and body before returning deliberately to her eyes. His tall strong body exuding so much heat he could practically have started a fire all on his own, he leaned closer yet. "You wouldn't."

Aware she was tingling all over and he hadn't even touched her yet, Amy offered him a sassy smile, pretending an ease she couldn't begin to feel. "Why not?" She moved closer, so the two of them were squaring off next to the telephone on the kitchen wall.

"Because you're a hearts-and-flowers kind of girl." Nick reached past her to pick up his mug. He lifted it to his lips and took a swallow of the steaming liquid. "The type who waits to be pursued and romanced under just the right circumstances," he continued as if he wasn't the least bit interested in exploring the sizzling physical and emotional chemistry between them. "Not the kind who would make the first move with a man."

Which was, Amy thought, perhaps the problem. In business she had no trouble mustering up the courage to do whatever was necessary to achieve her goals, but in her romantic life, she was a marshmallow. Or at least she had been up to now. But she couldn't continue on the way she had, waiting for her very own Mr. Right to come along and sweep her off her feet. If she wanted to be happy, if she wanted to be involved with the man she wanted to be involved with, she was going to have to get off her keister and do something about it. "So in other words you would ignore your attraction to me in order to do business with my mother?" she said softly and disparagingly, making her feelings on his decision very clear.

Nick's lips tightened as he set his now-empty coffee mug on the counter beside her. "I never said I was attracted to you."

Amy lounged against the counter and folded her arms in front of her as if she hadn't a care in the world. She inclined her head, mocking him with both her posture and the look on her face. "You're telling me you're not?" she taunted. Used to fending off advances from men right and left for as far back as she could remember, Amy didn't quite know what to do with Nick's hot-and-cold, I-want-you-but-I'm-not-going-to-do-anything-about-it behavior.

Nick was silent. He adapted a no-nonsense stance, arms folded, legs braced apart, which would have been very intimidating had Amy allowed it. She didn't. He narrowed his gray eyes at her and began to erect an emotional forcefield around himself once again. "We're both adults here, Amy," he said at last.

*No kidding,* Amy thought, knowing there was nothing innocent and childlike about what she wanted to do with him. "Adult enough to ignore the way we're feeling," she presumed, determined not to follow his lead and refuse to acknowledge her real instincts, as he was obviously doing.

"Right," he said, looking increasingly annoyed.

"Maybe you are," Amy tossed back lightly and flirtatiously, "but I'm not." And then she did what she had never before done in her life. She made the first move and delivered the first kiss. To her acute disappointment, however, Nick was motionless in her arms, his lips unresponsive as stone. Her heart pounding, face flushed, she drew back, wondering how something that seemed so right could have turned out so wrong.

"Finished?" Nick said dryly as Amy ran a hand through her tousled hair, keeping it off her face.

Amy gulped and did her best to hold her humiliation at bay. "I guess so," she returned in a low flip tone, deciding Nick didn't need to know just how disappointed and mixed-up she was.

"Good," Nick said, closing the distance between them. Hands on her waist, he shifted her back against the counter, then held her there firmly, her slender body pressed against the hard length of his. "Because there is something you should know," he continued, bracing his hands on the countertop on either side of her. "If there is going to be any kissing between the two of us, it will be at my behest, and it won't be for show, and it won't be to prove a point."

"Then how will it be?" Amy demanded breathlessly, splaying her hands across his chest.

"Like this," Nick said. And then he wrapped both arms around her, fused his lips to hers in a combination of want and need, and kissed her the way she had always wanted to be kissed but never been had been. He kissed as if he meant to possess her in both body and heart, until she was as lost in the miracle of it as he. Needing to be closer yet, she stood on tiptoe and wrapped her arms around his neck. Her lips parted beneath the insistent pressure of his, and she melted against him in boneless pleasure, feeling his hardness pressing against her. Passion swept through her, weakening her knees, making her insides turn hot and melting, and then all was lost in a storm of their own making.

NICK HAD KISSED Amy to both teach her a lesson and dissuade her from ever again starting anything she wasn't well prepared to finish. He did not want to be used just to make a point with her family—that she could live life her own way or choose her own beaux no matter how unacceptable they might be to the Deveraux family.

What he hadn't expected was that she would feel so deliciously warm and right in his arms that he didn't want to let her go. Or that, instead of stiffening in shocked resistance—as he had expected her to do, given the way this embrace had started—or trying to fight him off, that she would surge against him and open her mouth to the plundering exploration of his lips and tongue. She tasted sweet and feminine, her body soft and accessible, her spirit as filled with yearning and need as his own. All they had done was kiss, and already he wanted to make love to her. And damn, if she didn't seem to want the same thing, Nick thought, all too aware that he had started this little experiment to push her away and had ended up feeling as recklessly aroused as Amy. And that was something he couldn't—wouldn't—allow to happen again, Nick warned himself sternly, forcing himself to remove his lips from the tempting surrender of hers.

Not without risking that this experimental embrace would turn into something more than a brief, meaningless fling.

Aware his heart was pounding every bit as hard as hers, Nick lifted his lips and stepped back and away. "The next time I'm not going to stop with just a kiss," he warned, hoping to use words to shake some sense into her in a way that his actions hadn't managed. He looked at Amy sternly. "The next time, if there is a next time, and to be ruthlessly honest I'm hoping there won't be," he told her, "we'll end up in bed."

Amy's turquoise eyes glittered with a mixture of excitement and pleasure. Her breasts rose and fell rapidly with each breath she took. Her soft lips curved in a satisfied smile as she asked, "And you think I'd mind that?"

The optimistic look on her face, which held so much hope for their future, only made him feel guiltier. Ignoring the tightness in his throat, Nick turned away from her hopelessly sunny smile. "If we play by my rules, you would," Nick told her calmly, aware that the kiss they had just shared was only going to make things worse between them. After this, he was going to keep wanting her, and not just as a baby-sitting partner. And unless he missed his guess, Amy was going to keep wanting him, too.

She moved close enough that he could smell the tantalizing apple-blossom fragrance of her hair. She watched as Nick poured himself another cup of the hot strong coffee. "And your rules are…?"

Nick took a bracing sip of coffee and pretended a coldheartedness he couldn't begin to feel. "Never be there in the morning," he recited casually. "It prevents a lot of awkward moments. Never pretend it's going to be anything more than what it is—a strictly sexual relationship," he continued, ignoring the flash of hurt on her face. "And last but not least, keep things practical, honest. That way people won't get hurt."

Amy scrutinized his face. "I think plenty of women have been hurt by your parameters, Nick," she said, appearing no less determined to reform him. "They've just had too much pride to let you know it."

"If that's true," Nick said evenly, "it's the last thing I ever intended."

Amy shrugged offhandedly. "So change your outlook and your way of doing things," she murmured.

"Can't do that," Nick said. Because then he really would end up hurting her.

Amy blew out an exasperated breath and planted both hands on her hips. "I figured as much," she returned in a sassy tone that quickly had him wanting to take her in his arms—and possess her sexually and in every other way—all over again. "Not that it matters, you know," Amy continued in a low baiting tone, "because I have rules, too, you know."

Nick lifted a curious brow, refusing to let her exasperate him. "And they are?"

She smiled with admirable idealism. Her voice as gentle and soothing as a silk ribbon against his skin, she advised wisely, "If you make love to someone, you need to use more than just your body. You need to use your heart."

A nice theory—except when it came to him. With him, all she would be guaranteed was eventual disappointment and hurt. And she didn't deserve that. In an attempt to infuriate her—and hence push her away—he let his gaze skim her deliberately, provocatively. "What else?"

Amy closed the distance between them and stuck a finger in his chest. "Having sex with someone is as physically intimate as it gets in this life. When you're that close to someone, feelings are involved, whether you like it or not, Everton." Her lips curving sweetly, she went on to warn, "You can deny them. You can ignore them. But you *cannot* make them go away through sheer force of will."

"Maybe for you, it's that way," Nick countered, irritated to find her getting under his skin, after all.

Amy gave him one last telling look. "It's that way for everyone, Nick. Everyone." Finished, she spun on her heel and walked away.

To Nick's relief, business dominated the rest of the morning. Business was the one thing he could always handle.

"I thought Amy would be here this morning," Grace told Nick when she breezed in for the meeting they had scheduled before she'd left the cottage the night before.

Ignoring the plastic rattle Dexter was shaking in his face, Nick shifted his nephew to his other arm and reached around to close the door behind Grace. "Amy had to do a living-room consultation for someone this morning and then meet with the workmen who are going to paint her aunt Winnifred's carriage house." Nick had been both relieved and sorry to see Amy go. He had the feeling that had she stayed, the two of them would have ended up either arguing or kissing again. Neither was a comfortable option for him. And yet the loneliness he felt when he was apart from her was even worse.

"When will she be back?" Grace asked.

"She thought around noon." In the meantime Nick had his own work to do, along with the baby-sitting duties. "So if you're ready, we can go ahead and get started."

"Actually," Grace said with a smile, dropping her handbag and briefcase on the floor next to the sofa, "what I'd really like is to hold that nephew of yours. Would you mind?"

"Not if Dexter doesn't," Nick said as he transferred Dexter to Grace's waiting arms. Smart enough to know a good thing when he saw one, Dexter gurgled and snuggled against the chic older woman. "So, Nick, tell me what you're proposing," Grace said in a crisp businesslike tone as she tenderly smoothed the tufts of sparse hair on the infant's head.

Nick sat down on the sofa and laid out the papers he'd prepared upside down, so Grace could see them from where she was standing. "I had some focus-group testing done on your old *Rise And Shine, America!* shows. As you can see—" Nick pointed to the graphs and reports of viewer comments "—your homemaker segments tested the best because they were the funniest."

Grace settled into the rocking chair with Dexter and began to rock slowly and smoothly. "That's because I'm a complete idiot when it comes to anything domestic," she told Nick confidently. "I'm notoriously untalented in the kitchen and around the house." Grace smiled as Dexter waved his rattle in her face. "But I'm hoping that will change now that I'm on hiatus and have more leisure time."

"Not too much, I hope," Nick said, getting up to get a flannel baby blanket to lay across Grace's shoulder so that her dress would not be marred by saliva or spit-up. "At least not too quickly," Nick amended as he sat back down on the sofa. "Because that's what I want you to do for the syndicated TV show I'm proposing," he concluded.

Grace's lips curled in a self-effacing smile. "Make a fool of myself?"

"Inform, instruct, educate and entertain," Nick corrected, making certain Grace Deveraux knew this show was nothing she would ever have to feel embarrassed about. In fact, he hoped to make her feel very proud. "I want you to do a thirty-minute show five times a week that covers everything from decorating to cooking to gardening to child care to personal growth."

Her expression blissful as she continued to cuddle the infant in her arms, Grace pressed a kiss to the top of Dexter's head. She shot Nick an intrigued glance and murmured, "That sounds…far-ranging."

"And interesting."

Grace was silent as she continued to cuddle Dexter as affectionately and tenderly as if he were her long-awaited grandchild. "I'd want it to be filmed right here in Charleston," she warned, like the savvy businesswoman she was.

Nick frowned, thinking of the difficulties that would present. It would mean finding a soundstage. Finding experienced staff who lived here or were willing to relocate. "That could be a problem," he warned.

Grace looked at him steadily. "You're a smart man," she said pleasantly. "I trust you to be able to make it work."

Nick could tell by the look on her face that Grace Deveraux's demand was a deal breaker. The veteran TV host wanted to be near her family after years of living several states away. She wasn't going to agree to anything that would have her living and working in New York, Los Angeles or Chicago—the three cities where Nick already owned soundstages and had shows in production. "Okay," he conceded at last figuring it would be worth whatever hoops he had to jump through to sign her to his company. "What else?"

Grace smiled as Dexter dropped his rattle onto her lap and grabbed at the pretty broach pinned to the shoulder of her dress. "I want you to be the executive producer," Grace told Nick calmly pressing another kiss to the top of Dexter's head. "And I'm not talking about your being just a figurehead. I'd want you on the set, behind the camera, personally talking it up to stations."

Nick sat back with a frown. "I don't do that anymore."

Grace leveled a telling look at him. "If you want me to sign with your company, you will."

Nick had to admit he wouldn't mind getting back in the trenches for the right project. This was the right project. "All right, but I have demands, too."

"Such as?" Grace asked.

"I want a minimum two-year, five-hundred-show commitment from you. You'll have to actively promote the show and give my company a percentage of the profits of any merchandise the show generates— like books or magazines or whatever. The specifics, of course, will be worked out by our lawyers."

"I can live with that," Grace said thoughtfully after a moment.

"I'd want to get started right away," Nick warned her. In business it was important to strike while the iron was hot. Right now, there was a lot of public interest in Grace Deveraux and in whatever project she wanted to do next.

"The sooner the better as far as I'm concerned," Grace agreed as the front door to the cottage opened and shut.

Nick and Grace glanced up as Amy walked in.

Amy looked from one to the other. Nick noted she didn't seem particularly happy to see him with her mother. Hoping to smooth over any tension, he explained what they had agreed upon.

"Sounds exciting. It'll be especially nice to have you staying in Charleston," Amy said, leaning down and giving her mom a hug.

"I think so, too." Grace stood and returned the embrace with one arm, then glanced at the clock. "Oh, dear, I'm going to be late."

Grace stood and handed Dexter back to Nick.

Amy watched as her mother picked up her handbag and briefcase. "I was hoping you could stay and have lunch with us," Amy said.

Grace tucked the proposal Nick handed her into her briefcase and replied, distractedly, "I'd love to, dear, but I've got a yoga session with Paulo, and then the two of us are going to lunch together after that."

Amy tensed. "I wish you'd stop seeing him."

Wrong thing to say to your mother, Nick thought, as Grace stiffened. "Amy..."

"I mean it, Mom," Amy continued, ignoring her

mother's warning glare. "You can't be serious about him!"

Grace lifted a delicate brow. "And why not?" she demanded.

"Because he's so much younger than you, that's why!" Amy burst back.

The elegant lines of Grace Deveraux's face tightened. "Your father sees younger women."

A fact that obviously hurt Amy, too, Nick noted sympathetically.

Amy regarded her mother all the more defiantly. "He's not serious about them, either," she said.

Grace looped her handbag over her shoulder and headed for the door. "We deserve to have social lives, Amy."

Amy rushed to cut her off, stepping between her mother and the door. "You deserve to be back together," Amy said.

Grace touched Amy's shoulder. "Honey, that just isn't going to happen," she said gently.

Amy's lips twisted in exasperation. "If you two would just try...."

Grace dropped her hand and stepped back. Nick noted she was beginning to look angry with her only daughter. "You already tried to engineer a reconciliation between us, by setting up a surprise 'date' for us on the family yacht, and it just didn't happen," Grace warned sternly. "I want you to promise me you won't do anything like that again."

"I can't promise you," Amy retorted emotionally,

still standing between her mother and the exit. Tears welled in her eyes and her voice grew thick. "I see you and Dad just throwing everything away. And it tears me apart."

"Well, it tears us apart to have to keep explaining to you that our divorce was final years ago," Grace returned just as emotionally.

As soon as Grace left, Nick closed the distance between himself and Amy. "You shouldn't pressure your mother that way. She has a good reason for feeling the way she feels."

Amy glared at him, resenting the interference. "How do you know?"

Sensing she needed someone to talk sense into her, and it might as well be him, Nick returned calmly, "Because people don't get divorced or decide not to ever marry again for no reason."

Amy lifted her chin defiantly. "I don't care what either of them say, Nick. They still love each other. They're just too stubborn to admit it. Which is why I have to keep trying to get them to see reason and give their relationship another try."

He knew Amy had her parents' best interest at heart, but he didn't want to see her get hurt. Right now, if she continued on the same track, she would be. "Even if your mother would rather that you not?" Nick asked.

Amy went to the kitchen and removed the pitcher of lemonade from the refrigerator. "I can't help it. The world would be a much better place if it weren't full of quitters like my mom and dad who, after getting hurt once, refuse to put their hearts on the line again.''

Nick followed, a sedate Dexter in his arms. He wondered what Amy would think of him, if she knew how he had given up—on love, marriage, home and family. Would she understand why he had reacted the way he had? Would she believe the only way he had been able to go on was by knowing that he would never have to suffer such hurt or let anyone down like that again? Or would she think what he sometimes thought in the dark of night, that he was a coward for refusing to try again. And a screwup, not in his professional life, but where it counted most.

Not that it mattered what Amy thought, Nick reminded himself sternly, since he had no intention of getting involved with her, now or at any time in the future. No, the only help he wanted from Amy was with Dexter. And one other thing. ''I need a favor from you,'' he said as she poured two glasses of lemonade.

Amy lifted a brow as she handed him a glass. ''What kind of favor?'' she asked.

Aware it had gotten a lot warmer inside the cottage since Amy had returned, Nick drank thirstily of the icy liquid. ''If I'm going to be working here in Charleston, I'm going to need an office, and the sooner the better.'' He drained his glass, then set it aside. ''Do you know any commercial Realtors?''

Amy inclined her head thoughtfully. ''Connor

Templeton, Daisy Templeton's brother, buys and sells hotels, office buildings and restaurants. He could probably get you what you need.''

"Got his number?" Nick asked.

Amy nodded and went to get it. Two phone calls later Nick had an appointment to see a property that was available now and would probably meet his needs. "Why don't you and Dexter come with me?" Nick asked on impulse.

Amy flushed pink as they spread a blanket out on the floor and gently put Dexter down in the middle of it. "You don't need my opinion."

"Actually I do." Nick sat down beside her and Dexter. "I want you to decorate it for me."

"As soon as possible?" Amy guessed as Dexter waved his arms, pulled up his legs and tried repeatedly to grasp his toes.

"Like by the end of business tomorrow," Nick specified, knowing there was no time like the present to get everything in place. Before Grace Deveraux changed her mind or was convinced—by her business managers—to field other offers that were coming her way right now.

Amy did a double take, apparently amazed at the speed with which he was proceeding. "You don't waste any time, do you?" she said dryly.

Thinking how pretty Amy looked with the sunlight shimmering in her dark hair, Nick shrugged. "I know what I need and want. Why mess around?"

Amy's mysterious smile grew even softer and more alluring. "Indeed."

"So will you do it?" Nick said.

Amy studied him wordlessly. Nick could see she was debating the wisdom of conceding to his demands. Eventually, as he'd hoped would be the case, the businesswoman in her won out over the would-be girlfriend. "Sure," Amy said after a moment. "Why not?"

NICK WAS PLEASED to discover that Connor Templeton was every bit as knowledgeable about commercial real estate as Amy claimed. By the time Amy, Nick and Dexter arrived at his office in downtown Charleston, Connor had all the facts and figures ready and the necessary paperwork ready to go. The four of them went over to check out the property. Finding it everything he had asked for and more, Nick signed the lease. "I'm also going to need a soundstage," Nick said, handing the pen back to Connor while Amy walked the rooms, a sleeping Dexter in her arms. "Probably ten thousand square feet, with room for several different sets and ample storage and editing booths.

"That will be harder to come by," Connor said, entering a notation in his PalmPilot. "But I'll get on it right away." Looking every bit the affable, successful thirty-something businessman he was, Connor turned to Amy and said, "By the way, I talked to Daisy on the way over, and she said to tell you she's got the photos ready for you to look at. She can bring them over this evening, if you want. Just give her a call.''

"Thanks, Connor." Amy smiled. "I will."

Connor left. Amy and Nick were alone with Dexter in the empty fifth-floor suite. "Well, what do you think?" Nick asked Amy as she settled Dexter into his carrier/car seat and strapped him in.

Amy moved away from the soundly sleeping baby. "It's a good location. Convenient to the freeway, the business district and downtown. And the rooms are spacious." She raked her teeth across her lower lip as she looked around. "Any idea what you want to do with them?"

Nick nodded and gestured at the room closest to the small L-shaped foyer. "I want this room to be my office."

"And not the reception area," Amy ascertained. She took a notepad out of the pocket of her white linen blazer.

"I'm not going to have a secretary at this location, so no."

"What about this room?" Amy walked into the second. It was large and square, with a wall of floor-to-ceiling tinted-glass windows.

"It'll be my personal space." Nick looked around, still unable to shake the memory of the kisses they had shared that morning, of the way Amy had felt and smelled and tasted, of the way she had first put the moves on him and then kissed him back, with absolutely nothing held in check. He felt stunned by her ability to draw him into her emotional life. And saddened that it was a place he wasn't going to be able to stay. Not and keep his own emotional armor intact. Turning away from her, Nick continued listing his demands. "So I'm going to need a comfortable sofa bed, entertainment center and an armoire for my clothing."

If Amy was surprised by his desire to stay there, instead of a hotel, she didn't show it. "Any instructions for the bath and shower?" she asked calmly. Nick knew there wasn't much she could do with them. The facilities were cramped and utilitarian, meant more for emergency, not daily use.

"Just make sure it's outfitted with everything I need," Nick said. "Towels, mats, laundry hamper, whatever else you think."

Amy nodded. "What kind of style do you prefer for the other two rooms?" she asked. When Nick hesitated, not sure how to answer that—Did he even have a style he preferred?—Amy continued questioning him persistently. "Do you want something that's sleek and modern? Or something with a lot of leather and heavy wood furniture?"

"You choose."

"What's your favorite color?"

"Don't have one," Nick said automatically.

Amy's eyes widened in a mixture of surprise and disbelief. "What color is your living room at home?" she asked.

Nick shrugged, beginning to resent the personal direction her questions had taken. He had hired her precisely so he wouldn't have to think about things like this—wouldn't have to care about these domestic details. Beyond that, he didn't give a damn about where he stayed. And since the catastrophe that had changed his life, never would again. Aware she was still waiting—rather impatiently, it seemed—for an answer, Nick said flatly, "I don't have one."

She regarded him skeptically, beginning to get a little piqued. "You don't have a living room?" she repeated in mock indignation.

Nick looked at her. "I don't have a home."

# Chapter Eight

Amy stared at Nick. "You don't have a home," she repeated, incredulous.

"Right."

Sure she had somehow misunderstood what he was trying to say to her, Amy narrowed her eyes and said, "You mean you're between residences."

"No," Nick countered. "I mean I don't own one."

Amy blinked. The way he was suddenly challenging her was making her angry. It was also enticing and intriguing her. She had known from the outset that Nick Everton was a very complicated man. Beneath his smooth-spoken, soft-cavalier exterior, beat the heart of a businessman and the soul of a devoted brother and uncle. That he refused to admit he was a family man stymied her. Anyone with as much love as Nick clearly had to give must want a family of his own, at least at some point. Yet Nick denied that. Why? "Then where do you live?" Amy asked curiously, aware she would give anything to know what made him tick.

"Wherever I'm working at the time," Nick said offhandedly, shooting an attentive look at the still-soundly-sleeping Dexter in the infant carrier in the corner. "I have offices in New York City, Los Angeles, Miami, Chicago, Atlanta and now Charleston. I have sleeping quarters in my office in all of them, except the one in New York City. When I'm there, I usually stay in a hotel because there's no shower in the office suite I have there."

"And that's okay with you?" Amy asked in disbelief, thinking how cold and empty that way of life must be. She loved going home to her own cozy abode. Creating a place to live and love was one of the great pleasures—and challenges—of life. But, judging by the closed expression on his face, Nick apparently didn't see it that way. Unlike her, he didn't care where he hung his hat at the end of the day.

Nick lifted his shoulders in an indifferent shrug and kept his eyes leveled on hers. "Why wouldn't it be okay with me?"

Amy could think of lots of reasons. Trying not to notice how much Nick's nearness affected her—he was standing close enough she could feel the heat from his body and breathe in the soap and sandalwood of his cologne, close enough she could feel the undeniable sizzle of sexual attraction between them—she gestured vaguely. "People of your stature usually have several homes, real showplaces. I'd just figured you'd want that, too."

"Then you figured wrong." Nick looked irritated as he shoved a hand through his hair.

It didn't take a genius to see he was working overtime to hold her at arm's length emotionally. She had hoped their working together to decorate his new office/living quarters would be the start of their getting closer. Instead, he looked as if he wanted nothing more from her than a stop to any more questions about his personal life and or anything else on an intimate plane.

"Ready to go home?" Nick crossed to the infant carrier with the sleeping Dexter, picked it up and started for the door.

Hooking Dexter's diaper bag on one shoulder, her carryall on the other, Amy fell into step behind him. She knew Nick thought he'd succeeded in pushing her away, but that wasn't the case at all. "I've got to stop by my place first," she told him casually. "Check on the progress of the bathroom remodel, which, except for the final touches, should be about done. If you want," she said, their hands brushing as he handed her the keys, "you and Dexter could just drop me off there, and I could catch a ride back to Lola's later."

Because his arms were full of infant carrier and baby, Nick lounged against the wall and watched her lock up behind them. "We'll go with you," he said quietly.

As much as Amy was loath to inconvenience Nick and the baby, she had to admit that would be easier than prevailing on a member of her family, who would no doubt feel compelled to lecture her on the evils of staying under the same roof as Nick, or take a taxi all the way out to Lola's cottage. She smiled at him agreeably. "All right."

Traffic was light and the drive over was accomplished quickly, with most of the conversation taken up by the directions Amy was giving him to her place. By the time they arrived, Dexter was awake again and cooing happily.

While she got Dexter out of this car seat, Nick took a moment to survey her spacious Cape Cod home. "Nice paint," Nick remarked.

Amy liked the pale-peach siding with the snowy white trim and the dark-peach shutters and door as much as she liked the quiet residential neighborhood of sturdy two-story homes that had been built back in the fifties and had survived every hurricane since. "I think it's cheerful." Eager to see the nearly completed work, she placed Dexter in Nick's arms and bounded up the walk to the front porch. Behind her, Nick took his time, admiring the abundant flowers, neatly trimmed shrubbery and palmetto trees in her front yard. "How long have you lived here?" he asked.

Amy shot him a look over her shoulder as she unlocked the front door. "Since shortly after I graduated from college, so it's been about seven years, I guess. It was the one time I used my trust fund—for the down payment," Amy admitted as she grabbed the day's mail out of the box next to her door and went inside. "I really wanted a home of my own and couldn't afford it, otherwise."

"It looks like it's been completely redone," Nick said as he followed her into the foyer.

Amy nodded, proud of what she had accomplished in realizing the house's full potential. "I've been working on it room by room." A formal living room and dining room flanked the wood-floored foyer. Behind that were kitchen and family room. Upstairs was a study, a room that had been painted a sunny yellow and left completely bare in hopes of the child that was somewhere in her future, and further down the hall, a big master bedroom. "It used to have four bedrooms, but I got rid of one so I could enlarge the master bathroom and add more closet space," Amy explained, showing where she had taken out a wall as she led the way into the newly expanded master suite. "All that's left to be done besides the wallpapering is some caulking and touch-up painting, which should both be done tomorrow."

Nick looked around at the whirlpool tub that was big enough for two, glass-walled marble shower, twin sinks and built-in vanity. There was a walk-in closet on either side of the bath and a linen closet, as well. The room was in the process of being wallpapered in an abstract pastel print. Amy knew she had made a good choice there. She'd be able to change color schemes—both in the bath and in the adjoining master bedroom—at least a dozen times without having to change the wallpaper.

Nick nodded approvingly at the bath, then turned to the rest of the master bedroom. A big old-fashioned canopy bed with pale-peach damask linens faced the decorative-tiled fireplace she'd had put in. There was a cozy sitting area, with upholstered chairs, several beautiful plants and a beautiful seascape above an antique writing desk. "This is really nice."

Amy thought so, too. There was only one thing she needed to make her life there complete. Someone to love who also loved her back. Until now, she hadn't had anyone specific in mind. But now she could see someone there with her, enjoying the fruits of her labor. She could see Nick. "There's nothing like owning your own home, making it yours through and through. You ought to try it," Amy said softly. Maybe then he would understand what this place meant to her, what it meant to settle down.

"No," Nick said. His expression closing once again, he shifted baby Dexter higher in his arms. "That's not for me."

Amy sighed. So much for the subtle approach. If she was going to change Nick, she was going to have to try a lot harder.

AMY WAS USING her computer to work on a proposal for a client, Nick was out doing errands, and Dexter was sleeping when Lola called. "I'm so glad Chuck is doing well," Amy told Lola over the phone. Although it was barely suppertime in Charleston, it was almost midnight in Germany. "You must be so relieved, too," Amy continued happily.

"I really am." Lola paused, "The only good thing to come out of this is that Chuck's going to get several months' medical leave to recuperate, so he'll be coming back to the States with me as soon as he can travel. He'll finally get to see Dexter."

Amy knew how hard it had been for her friend to have her husband overseas on a covert mission with his military unit when their child was born. "Chuck must be looking forward to that," Amy enthused, knowing it must have been hard for Chuck, too, being separated from his family at such an extraordinary time.

"He really is. Speaking of which, how are things going there with Dexter? Has he had any more tummy aches?"

"No." Cradling the portable phone to her ear, Amy walked away from her desk and out onto the back porch. "We're being a lot more careful about burping him both during and after feedings, though, and adding the small amount of rice cereal first seems to have helped. He's not so hungry that he tries to gulp his bottle down anymore. It's easier to stretch his feeding out to the prescribed twenty minutes."

"That's good. What about Nick? How is he doing being around a baby?"

"Just fine." Amy bent to take a load of baby clothes out of the drier. She tumbled them into a basket. "Why do you ask?"

"No reason," Lola said swiftly.

Her antennae on alert, Amy sat down on a chaise and began to fold a stack of infant undershirts. "Does Nick not like babies?"

"Well...he usually just doesn't want to be around them," Lola said after a moment.

"Why not?" Amy asked as she mated a pair of blue booties. As far as she could tell, Nick adored being around his nephew.

"Nothing. I really shouldn't have said anything."

O-kay, Amy thought. Not about to let the conversation end without at least some answers, Amy speculated bluntly, "I guess it probably has something to do with the reason he doesn't own a home, either." After all, there had to be some reason an obvious family man like Nick so totally resisted the idea of marriage, home and kids. If anyone knew what it was, besides Nick, it was probably his kid sister.

There was a silence on the other end. "How did you know that?" Lola asked finally, her surprise evident.

*I didn't for certain,* Amy thought, glad her fishing expedition had turned up something valuable, *until now*.

"Surely," Lola continued in a strangled tone, "Nick didn't confide in you about..."

"What?" Amy prodded, more curious than ever.

"Never mind," Lola replied hastily.

"What is Nick not telling me, Lola?" Amy asked bluntly, figuring as long as she was sharing quarters with him and interested in him romantically she deserved to know.

"I really can't discuss Nick's private life with you, Amy. He'll tell you anything he wants you to know directly. Beyond that, well..." Lola's voice trailed off.

Amy sighed as she reached the bottom of the wicker basket. "You're making him sound very mysterious."

"That's not my intention," Lola protested.

Amy stacked the piles of sleepers, undershirts, playsuits and booties in the basket. "Then what *is* your intention?"

"To warn you away from him. Don't get involved with him, Amy. He'll only break your heart."

Amy sighed, exasperated. Now she was getting it from *his* family, too? "Why do you say that?"

"Nick's a great guy," Lola told her in a voice laced with friendship and affection. "If you need something, he'll find a way to achieve it or make it happen. But he doesn't let people near him, Amy, and he hasn't for a long time. Even I don't really know what's on his mind or in his heart most of the time. And I know you, Amy. You would never be happy being held at arm's length emotionally. And believe me, that's as close as you'd ever get to a man like Nick."

NICK KNEW THE MOMENT he walked in the door that something bad had happened in his absence. It was written all over Amy's face. "What's wrong?" he said.

"Nothing."

Amy placed a thick bath towel on the kitchen table and then crossed to the kitchen sink.

Nick put the grocery sacks containing several kinds of commercial infant formula on the kitchen counter.

"Then why are you looking so glum?" Nick asked.

"It's just been a long day," she said evasively.

*Right,* Nick thought. *And you're not the kind of woman who wears her heart on her sleeve.* All he knew for certain was that he hated seeing Amy look as if she had just lost her best friend.

Amy sent him a cheerful smile that was at odds with the troubled look in her eyes. "Lola called while you were gone. Chuck is continuing to improve. They think he'll be ready to come back to the States via air ambulance by the end of the week, if not sooner."

Nick nodded, relief pouring through him. He knew how much his sister loved her husband and what a good guy Chuck was. For a lot of reasons, it would have devastated them both had Lola lost him. Nick was glad she hadn't, that her life, anyway, would soon return to normal. "I can help her make the arrangements for that," he said.

Amy plucked Dexter out of the infant swing and carried him to the table. She laid him gently down on the folded towel next to the basin of water and began to undress him. "She said you had offered to do that before she left."

"Yes, I did." Prepared to help with Dexter's sponge bath, Nick rolled up his shirtsleeves.

"You're a good brother."

"Thanks." He tried to be. God knows, he didn't want to let Lola down.

Amy eased Dexter out of his terry-cloth playsuit and after glimpsing to make sure she was only dealing with wet pants, removed his disposable diaper. She shot Nick a sly glance. "You'd make a good father, too."

Nick tensed. He gave Amy a look that let her know she was venturing into forbidden territory. He slid a hand beneath Dexter's neck and smiled down at him. "How about I hold the little rascal while you wash?" Nick said, changing the subject smoothly.

"Okay." Nick admired Amy's touch as she dipped the washcloth into the water and washed Dexter's face with plain water. Finished, she rewet the cloth and squirted some liquid baby soap onto the middle of it. While Nick smiled down at Dexter, she rubbed the sides of the cloth together until a lather appeared and then gently washed the top and back of Dexter's head, his neck and chin. Rinsed it again, then continued working her way down Dexter's body. "Should I turn him over now?" Nick asked, when Amy had finished his front.

"If he'll tolerate it," Amy said.

Keeping one hand on Dexter's tummy, Nick gently turned him over. Dexter immediately put his weight on his forearms and pushed his head up, while Amy washed his shoulders and worked her way down his back, hips and legs. Before she could get him rinsed, Dexter shoved mightily against the towel and flipped over onto his back. Amy and Nick, who still had hold of Dexter, gasped with delight and surprise. Seeing the astonished looks on their faces, Dexter giggled with delight and waved his little arms and legs.

Noting that Amy looked every bit as pleased and proud as he was, Nick thought what a good and devoted mother she would make someday. "Did you know Dexter could do that?" Amy asked happily.

As Nick leaned in closer to help, he caught an intoxicating whiff of her apple-blossom perfume, and the softness of her silky hair brushed his chin. "Lola told me he had done it, but I hadn't seen it." Nick smiled and gently turned Dexter onto his stomach again, so that Amy could rinse the soap off his back. She had barely finished when Dexter gave another mighty push and flipped himself over again. He laughed and kicked his arms and legs delightedly.

"You really are something, little fella," Amy said, kissing Dexter's head tenderly.

Trying not to think how those same lips had felt against his not so long ago, Nick dried Dexter off as Amy went to get clean clothes.

"He sure is," Nick agreed, aware of the pounding of his pulse as Amy slid a disposable diaper under Dexter's bottom and fastened the edges shut.

"So why don't you want kids of your own?" Amy asked Nick, bringing the subject back around to him.

Once again, Nick felt as if he had stumbled into the fires of hell. His mood darkening, he looked her straight in the eye. "Because I wouldn't be a good father," he told her bluntly. "And I don't do anything I'm not good at."

For a long moment Amy said absolutely nothing in response. Yet Nick could tell by the way Amy was looking at him—as if he had grown two heads or something—that she wasn't going to accept his statement at face value and let it go at that. Which was the problem, he thought crankily, that came with sharing space with a person who valued personal intimacy with others as much as Amy did.

"I don't know how you can say that," she told him quietly at last. "You've been great with your nephew."

Guilt swept through Nick again in great daunting waves. "'Nephew' being the operative word here," he said huskily, wishing Amy would let the subject drop. But since she wouldn't, he had no choice but to explain. At least a little. "There's a difference between being responsible for someone for a very short period of time," he said, finding it suddenly necessary to put some physical distance between himself and Amy and Dexter both, "and taking on the responsibility for the rest of your life." He looked her straight in the eye. "I'm not worried about my ability to share baby-sitting duties with you for a week or so. I know I can handle that, even if it means my work suffers temporarily."

"It doesn't look to me like your work is suffering," Amy said as she smoothed baby powder over Dexter's body. "After all, you just talked my mother into doing her own television show for your production company. That's got to be some sort of coup in TV land."

Actually, it was, Nick thought with satisfaction. He was going to make a lot of money from this, not to mention the kudos he would get for taking a star player the network considered a hasbeen and turning her into the next Martha Stewart, albeit one with a more humorous touch. Nick shrugged off Amy's argument and regarded her steadily. "It's going to take every ounce of energy I have to get her show up and running, and do the rest of my work," Nick said. "So all I'm going to have time for is work." He was using the same lame excuse that had effectively worked to turn off women in the past.

But Amy wasn't buying it, Nick noted unhappily.

"So hire more assistants," Amy said.

"I like my life the way it is, Amy," Nick said stonily.

Amy looked at Nick as if she didn't believe that. Not for one red-hot second. And more, resented him for trying to pull one over on her. Finished dressing Dexter, she lifted him in her arms. The baby giggled and immediately reached for a fistful of Amy's hair. "I'm going to feed him and put him down for the night," she said, then walked away from Nick without another word.

"SO HOW MUCH LONGER are you going to give me the silent treatment?" Nick asked in frustration, his low voice underscoring every word, as the two of them finished their dinner of take-out chicken and got up to do the dishes. He had always hated letting someone down. Letting Amy down, the way he obviously had, was a million times worse.

Amy bit her lower lip. "I'm not giving you the silent treatment," she said, then averted her eyes.

Nick grasped her chin and made her meet his gaze. "I guess you're right," he said as he took the container of coleslaw from her hands and put it aside. "You did say at least three sentences while we ate. 'Yes,' 'No' and 'I don't know.'"

A pulse throbbed in Amy's neck as she regarded him silently, clearly wanting to be able to open up to him, but not quite able to. Probably because of what her ex-boyfriend had put her through, Nick thought. By her own admission, she had spent years hoping Kirk would change—and want the same things out of life that she wanted—only to have her hopes for the future dashed in the end, when Kirk couldn't or wouldn't do as she wished. "I couldn't think of anything to say," she returned quietly.

Nick studied the unhappiness in her eyes. And once more found himself wishing he could simply kiss all her past disappointments away. Knowing that wasn't an option, however, if the two of them were to keep from getting even further emotionally involved with each other, Nick stepped back a pace and concentrated on putting the leftover food away. "Or anything I would want to *hear* you say?'' he queried softly.

Amy snapped clear plastic lids on plastic-foam tubs of mashed potatoes and gravy and shoved them into the refrigerator. ''I don't want to fight with you, Nick.''

Nick added the leftover box of chicken and biscuits and coleslaw to the shelves. All too aware how very pretty Amy looked in the snug-fitting turquoise shirt and shorts, he shut the refrigerator door with the flat of his hand and said, ''Right. You'd rather just disapprove in silence.''

Amy sighed. ''I can't help feeling what I feel.''

Nick studied the fire in her eyes and the new color in her golden skin. ''Which is?''

Amy took a breath, the motion gently lifting her breasts, and glided closer in a drift of apple-blossom perfume. She propped her hands on her waist and tilted her head back to look into his eyes as she replied, ''That you're lying to me or yourself or maybe both, when it comes to the prospect of your having kids. And why you can or can't do that.''

Trying without success not to notice how soft and kissable and bare her lips were, or recall just how sweetly and tenderly she had kissed him back the one time he had let his feelings get the better of him, Nick reluctantly tore his gaze from her mouth and focused once more on the shimmering resentment in her eyes. ''So in other words,'' he guessed, aware his own temper was beginning to flare at the continued chill in her attitude and the growing disapproval on her face, "you think I should forget my own reservations to the contrary, and marry and have kids."

Amy came forward, not stopping until they were toe-to-toe. "I think you'd be a lot happier if you had a family, yes," Amy retorted vehemently. "Anyone would be."

"I have a family," Nick said, aware this was the first time he had ever seen her angry with him. And that she looked very pretty when she was angry. "I have Lola and Chuck and now Dexter."

Amy propped her hands on her hips, the indignant action jiggling her breasts even more. "You know what I mean." She blew out a long exasperated breath and pushed her silky mahogany hair from her face with the heel of one hand. "A marriage partner to go through life with. And children of your very own."

As always, the thought of marrying again, of opening himself up to that kind of hurt—or worse, failing to protect those closest to him again—had Nick's gut clenching. "Now see, therein lies the flaw in your thinking," Nick replied passionately. "Not everyone wants what you want, Amy. Nor is what's right for you right for everyone else." Even though if he ever was to marry again, he could only see himself marrying and having children with one woman. And that woman was standing right in front of him. Mule-stubborn and idealistic and sweetly vulnerable at heart.

"Everyone needs to be really close to someone, Nick," Amy retorted passionately, defiantly holding his gaze and standing her ground. Sounding as if she didn't give a hoot what was in his past, only in his future, Amy continued emotionally, "And the people who say otherwise are lying to themselves."

She was right about that, Nick admitted reluctantly. Because, although he still wasn't interested in putting himself in a situation where he could fail again, he did want to be close to Amy. As close as it was possible to be. The question was, would what he wanted ever be enough for her? And was it fair to even ask— given the newly passionate way she was regarding him? Or was he just begging for more trouble even thinking about getting temporarily involved?

Struggling to contain the rising heat in his groin, Nick kept his distance and reminded her gruffly, "It takes all kinds, Amy. Everyone needs to follow their own path to happiness."

"And what would yours be?" Amy taunted knowingly in a soft low voice that set his heart to racing.

Deciding there was only one way to end this question-and-answer session once and for all, Nick wrapped his arms around her and bent his head to hers. "Quite simply—" he said softly, truthfully "—this."

# *Chapter Nine*

Amy hadn't expected Nick to kiss her again. And she hadn't expected to respond to his kiss if he did. But the moment his lips touched hers, she was caught up in a tempest of emotion and yearning so intense she couldn't turn away. He might say he didn't want or need this, Amy thought, but his actions said otherwise. He held her so close they were almost one, and kissed her as if he would never get enough of her. Unable to turn away from such raw aching need, such undeniable tenderness and longing, she kissed him back with the same lack of restraint. Until all was lost in the wonder of the kiss, in the feel of his lips sensually discovering hers. His lower half was rigid with arousal. She moaned, shifting against him, and where he pressed against her, the ache increased with mesmerizing quickness. Her insides went liquid, and her knees weakened.

"Oh, Nick," Amy murmured as she pressed her breasts against his chest and boldly met him kiss for kiss. It had been so long since she had been desired like this. Never felt the potential to be close like this, to surrender like this. To love like this. For too long she had kept her need for passion, for enjoying the physical side of life, under wraps. For too long she had been afraid to risk. To open her heart again. To chance the kind of intimacy that would lead to a lifetime of love and commitment. No more.

"Tell me no," Nick whispered urgently against her parted lips as their continued embrace ignited a yearning and an ardor within her unlike any she had ever known.

The possessive look in his eyes made her catch her breath. "I'm telling you yes," she murmured back just as deliberately, wreathing her arms about his neck.

Without warning, the troubled look was back in his eyes. "You don't need me in your life," Nick said even as he was pressing her back against the wall, once again aligning the uncompromising hardness of his body against the soft give of hers. "You don't need this."

"I'll be the judge of that," Amy countered, rising on tiptoe to deliver another stirring kiss. She didn't know what it was about Nick, she thought as they breathlessly moved apart, but he made her want to take the risks she had never dared to take and be the kind of woman she had always been afraid to be. Until now.

Looking as entranced with her as she was with him,

Nick sifted his fingers through her hair, tilting her head up to his and staring down into her eyes. "I want to make love to you," he whispered, tracing the bow shape of her lip with the pad of his thumb. Even though, as Amy could plainly see, there was some reason Nick felt he should not.

Another shiver of excitement went through her. Again, she threw caution to the wind and went with what her heart was telling her to do. "I want to make love with you, too," she confessed huskily.

At her permission, Nick's eyes darkened with the depth of his desire. Wordlessly, he swept her up into his arms and carried her out onto the back porch. Set her down next to the cushioned chaise and slid his hands beneath the hem of her shirt, his palms erotically caressing her skin, his lips pressing delicious kisses down her throat. "You're going to have to tell me what you want."

That was easy, Amy thought, already tingling from head to toe. She looked into his eyes. Toes curling in sweet anticipation, her bare feet dug into the wooden floor. "Just you."

He smiled in the moonlit darkness of the porch. As her shirt came off and then her bra, the warm breeze caressed her skin. He smiled with sheer masculine pleasure as his eyes caressed her breasts, taking in the full globes. Her nipples beading and aching, she felt wicked and sensual, and more desired than she ever had been in her life. And he hadn't even touched her yet.

"Ah, Amy," Nick teased warmly as he bent her backwards over his arm and dropped his head, "you can do better than that." His hands found her breasts, molding and lifting their shape, even as his lips fastened on her nipples, which tingled beneath the gentle ministrations of his lips and tongue. Lower still, Amy felt a melting sensation, a weakening of her limbs. Her back arched, her thighs parted. Closing her eyes, she laced her hands about his neck. She swayed, almost drunkenly, against him, hardly able to believe how much she wanted him. They had barely started and already she was teetering on the edge of blissful oblivion. She wanted him to catch up. She pushed away from him on trembling knees, straightened. "Nick."

He merely grinned and hooked his arm about her waist. "Tell me," he said.

Amy guided his hand to the button at her waist. He undid it. Waited.

Able to feel his arousal pressing against her middle, she moved his fingers to the zipper of her shorts. Smiling, he undid that, too. The next thing Amy knew, she was pushing off her shorts herself, stepping out of her bikini panties. Wanting to touch him, see him, too, she reached for the fly of his slacks, even as his gaze worshiped her in the shadowy light. "I'm not going to be the only one naked here," she said.

"You're not," he said, and she helped him remove his shirt and then his shoes, socks, slacks and briefs.

Able to see how much he wanted her in the hard

throbbing length of him, the bunched muscles, the scorching heat of his skin, Amy linked her arms about his neck, stood on tiptoe and murmured, "Better," against his lips.

"Much," Nick agreed as he smoothed his hands down her back, tracing the dip of her waist, the flare of her hips, the small of her spine, before moving lower still. Amy caught her breath as his palm slid through the nest of curls to the apex of her thighs and the feminine heart of her. "Like this?" he murmured, stroking her with his fingers and then his palms.

Amy gasped at the butterfly touches that soon had her shuddering and found him, too. He was hot, hard and ready. "Oh, yes," she said, as Nick began to kiss her again, tenderly at first, then with growing urgency. The next thing she knew she was dropping to the chaise, Nick's tall strong body draped over hers. His hands slid beneath her, and then he was moving downward, his lips ghosting over her belly, pressing lower still, finding the soft flesh of her inner thighs, then the tops of her knees, her calves, ankles. Amy's breath came jerkily as he began working his way slowly up again. "Nick," she moaned as he cupped her breasts with his hands, brushed his thumbs across the tips, once and then again and again.

"I'm not hurrying," he whispered as he parted her knees and slid between them. "And neither are you." He slid his palms beneath her thighs, lifting her up, forcing her open, and his lips touched her intimately. Amy gasped as his tongue moved up, in and then the

stars above them exploded in a million twinkling
lights. And it still wasn't enough. Not nearly, Amy
thought as she slipped from beneath Nick and
changed places with him. Determined to give as much
as she got, she found him with her lips and tongue.
Loving the strong hard feel of him, she traced his flat
nipples, the dip of his sternum and the width of his
shoulders. His chest rose and fell with every breath
he took, and her own body still damp and tingling,
Amy worked her way downward. Past the silken muscle and curly hair that arrowed past his navel to the
flat sexy abdomen and his abundant sex. Wanting him
to want her the way she wanted him, she cupped the
fertile part of him with one hand and stroked the
length of him with the other. Base to tip and back
again. Over and again, around the edge, until he, too,
was quivering with need and repeatedly saying her
name.

The next thing Amy knew, Nick was reaching for
her again, flipping her so she was beneath him on the
chaise. The fierceness of their lovemaking swept them
both into its power. And then he was sliding over her,
lifting her and positioning her beneath him. Unable
to get enough of touching him and loving the way he
felt when poised over her, so hard and strong and
welcoming, Amy opened her legs and wrapped her
arms around him. Nick surged forward, pushing past
the resistance of a body that had gone far too long
without love, and then they were one. Pulsing, aching,
searching for the ultimate pleasure and release. Aware

she had never felt as close to anyone as she did to Nick at that moment, Amy closed her body around him and rocked against him. Until all coherent thought spun away. And then all was lost—and found—in the heat and wonder of the moment.

IT TOOK HIM about fifteen minutes of cuddling to realize what he had done. He hadn't just made love to or found physical solace in Amy's body. In his search for physical pleasure and release, he had someone involve her heart and soul, and more surprising, his. Otherwise, he wouldn't still be lying naked beside her on the narrow chaise, holding her close and stroking his hands through her hair. He would, as was his custom, already be up and out of here. Frowning guiltily—hadn't he promised himself he wouldn't hurt her?—Nick dropped his hold on her, and reluctantly got up.

Amy stayed where she was, snuggled on the chaise. There was just enough light filtering out from the house for Nick to be able to make out her face. Her expression both curious and wary, she watched him pull on his briefs and slacks. "I guess this is the part where you go home," she said in a voice that was, under the circumstances, more curious than hurt. "Only, you can't go home," she said in a softer, silkier voice. "Because for the moment, this is home, for both of us."

His conscience prickling all the more because he couldn't give her the kind of guaranteed protection and happily-ever-after love she deserved, Nick slipped on his shirt. He turned his glance away from Amy so he wouldn't be tempted to make wild, passionate, reason-robbing love to her again. Determined to behave in a way that would in no way, shape or form romanticize what had just happened between them, he regarded her politely and handed her the shirt that had been lying on the porch floor. "That was great."

Amy shot him a savvy look that said she wasn't buying his uninvolved act for a moment. "I'll say." She stretched languorously and made no move to cover her nakedness.

To his frustration, Nick felt himself growing hard again. Very hard. He swallowed, forcing himself not to react to her full rosy-tipped breasts, slender waist and long sexy legs. He couldn't afford to start thinking of this as more than a temporary thing, no matter how much he wanted to be part of her once again. "But we've got a busy day tomorrow," he concluded a lot more casually than he felt.

"So no more lovemaking tonight," Amy guessed with a mysteriously contented smile.

*Or ever, if I'm smart,* Nick thought. But not wanting to get into that right now, for fear of making an untenable situation even worse, Nick simply sucked in a bracing breath and said, "Right."

"Okay." Looking as thoroughly content as only a woman who had just been made very satisfying love to could, Amy sighed, stretched, stood. Her body looked lean and beautiful and sexy in the moonlight streaming in from one side of the porch. She flashed Nick a sly look. "Have it your way." She flashed him another smile, then pivoted and walked as sexy as you please into the house, through the living room and into the bedroom.

AMY KNEW THAT Nick was telling himself that what had happened between them meant nothing, but she knew better. *What had just occurred was not strictly physical,* she told herself firmly as she grabbed a robe and gown out of her suitcase and walked back across the hall to the bathroom. *And it wasn't an accident,* she continued her pep talk sternly as she poured some bubble bath into the tub and turned on the spigot, then watched the bubbles grow. *And it wasn't something destined never to happen again.*

No, Amy concluded as she stepped into the tub, leaned her head back against the rim and closed her eyes, Nick had made love to her like there was no other woman for him on earth. And she had made love to him the same way. Chemistry like that came along once in a lifetime, if you were lucky. She and Nick were lucky.

The question was, Amy wondered, how to make him see that, too.

On the surface of course, it was an impossible task, she admitted. She reached for a bath sponge and a bottle of her favorite apple-blossom cleanser. She poured the liquid soap onto the center of the sponge and then rubbed it across her shoulders and chest, the back of her neck, in soothing circular motions and continued thinking about the situation she found herself in.

For reasons she couldn't begin to fathom, Nick was certain he did not want marriage, family or even a place to call home. He thought satisfying work was enough to guarantee his happiness. And to a degree, Amy didn't dispute that. She derived immense satisfaction and pleasure from her work. But her work did not keep her warm at night, Amy recognized as she leaned forward to turn off the water and then continued soaping up her body with calm leisurely strokes. Her work did not make her feel loved or appreciated. It didn't push away the loneliness she sometimes felt or make her feel loved and wanted.

Making love with Nick, spending time with him, however, did give her all that and more, she acknowledged with a contented smile. When she was with Nick, she felt hopeful about the future. She felt as if all things were possible, as if there was no problem they couldn't solve as long as they worked at it together. And she sensed Nick felt that way, too, deep down.

The question was, how to get him to acknowledge that and open his heart and mind and life to love?

Right now, Amy had no answer. But her feminine instincts were telling her it was not only possible but probable. She just had to be patient. And not demand too much of him too soon. Nick was the kind of man who liked to be in the driver's seat of his own destiny. So she had to do what was hardest for her—let things happen at their own pace and not do any pushing.

"I DIDN'T HEAR Dexter get up during the night," Nick said when Amy came out of the nursery at dawn, a wide-awake Dexter propped on her hip. In fact, to his dismay he hadn't seen much of Amy since they had made love early the evening before and she had taken a long bath while he'd cooled his heels in the living room and tried to appear nonchalant, even though his concentration was blown to smithereens. Until she finally emerged looking and smelling so fragrant and sexy it had been all he could do to keep from apologizing for his loutish behavior and taking her in his arms, then make love to her again.

Not that Amy had seemed to expect anything of him, he admitted in fast-growing frustration. No, she had simply smiled at him and gathered up her work and then, dressed in another incredibly soft and feminine nightgown and robe, sat cross-legged on her bed. She concentrated on putting the proposal together for a client on her computer the rest of the evening. She'd come out of the bedroom at midnight to help change Dexter's diaper, give him a bottle and rock him back to sleep. Again, being as cordial and carefree as could be. That was the last time he had seen her.

"He slept right through, amazingly enough," Amy

said as she headed sleepily for the kitchen, her tousled hair falling like silk to her shoulders.

Although Nick had tossed and turned all night, while thinking about what he had and hadn't done right when it came to Amy, to his irritation, she appeared to have slept just fine. Better than fine, as a matter of fact, he noted grumpily. Beneath her surface composure, he'd never seen a woman look more loved than she did this morning. And he hadn't even given it his best shot, he thought resentfully. He hadn't made love to her again, although he had wanted to so much he'd hardly slept all night, and it had been all he could do not to go into the bedroom and entice her to join him again.

Oblivious to Nick's thoughts, Amy shut the freezer door. The bodice of her rose-colored spaghetti-strap nightgown slipped a little lower off her breasts, showing way too much of her smooth curves for Nick's comfort.

Not that he needed a glimpse of skin to remind him what she looked like. There was no way he was ever going to forget how beautifully her breasts were shaped, how soft her skin, how pretty and perfect her nipples were.

"Although I don't know how much longer that's going to be the case," Amy said as she tugged the lapels of her robe together in an attempt at modesty that did nothing to put out the fire of Nick's desire. She turned to him with a smile. "We're almost out of breast milk for him. In fact, this is the last container of it."

Nick shifted Dexter to his arms, then watched as Amy uncapped the bottle and put it in the microwave to thaw. He wished Amy didn't look so good in the early-morning sunlight, her cheeks flushed with sleep, her skin soft and glowing, and still smelling of the apple-blossom soap she favored. He wanted to think of her as a one-time sexual partner and nothing more. But here she was, ignoring the way he had walked out on her, being so sweet and nice and making it near impossible for him to keep the emotional barriers up.

"We have the commercially prepared formula I bought yesterday at the store," Nick said as Dexter beat his fists rhythmically on his bare chest.

Amy's dark brows knit. Her turquoise eyes gleamed with a troubled light. "But we don't know if Dexter will like it."

Nick winced as Dexter grasped his chest hair and twisted it in his tiny fists. "There are three different kinds, including a soy-based one." Nick tried, without success, to get Dexter to let go.

Amy came to the rescue, her hands brushing his chest as she worked to free Nick's hair from Dexter's hands. "It won't be the same as his momma's, though," she said. To Nick's relief she gently disengaged first one fist, then the other. Finished, she handed Dexter a terry-cloth toy to hold. Dexter grasped it awkwardly and put it to his mouth while

Nick worked to keep his eyes off Amy's luscious body and his mind on the conversation at hand.

"Maybe that's a plus," Nick said in a husky voice that sounded strained even to him. "Maybe the commercial formula will be just different enough to entice him."

Amy tilted her head in silent skepticism as she met and held his eyes. Nick hoped she didn't look downward, too. If she did, she would surely see that he wasn't as immune to her as he was pretending. "Let's hope that's the case," she said as the microwave dinged. "In the meantime I've got to get ready for work." Amy removed the bottle, shook it well and then tested it on her wrist. Finding it an acceptable temperature, she handed it to him with a smile. "So you get the first baby-sitting shift of the day."

TO NICK'S DISAPPOINTMENT, Amy didn't hang around once she was dressed and ready for work. As soon as she came out of the bedroom again, she grabbed her handbag and keys and headed for the door. "Aren't you going to have some breakfast?" Nick asked, following her. He'd made enough coffee for the two of them.

"I'll grab something later," Amy said, cell phone and briefcase in hand. She paused to kiss Dexter and pat his cheek, then smiled up at Nick as if she was the happiest woman on earth. Which didn't make sense, Nick thought, since they'd made love the evening before and then spent the night in separate beds.

Any other woman would have been so furious with him by now she wouldn't have been able to see straight. Any other woman would have kicked him out on his rear—and deservedly so.

"Right now, I'm off to get your office pulled together and then I'm going over to my aunt Winnifred's to see if the window treatments have been delivered for the carriage house yet. If they have—" Amy smiled enthusiastically "—I'm going to stay around and put them up myself."

Embarrassed to be feeling more like a neglected spouse than a disinterested one-time-only lover, Nick asked impatiently, "Can't you hire someone?"

"Sure." Amy shrugged. "But it would take another week. You rich people and these rush jobs." Amy winked, her good humor intact as she leaned forward to pat Dexter's cheek and give him a kiss goodbye. "Seems no one around here can wait for anything."

"Well, buddy, it looks like it's just you and me," Nick said after Amy left. But before the two of them could even get settled for some playtime, the phone rang. "Wonder who that could be," Nick said as he went to get the phone. It was his sister—with more good news. "The doctors said Chuck can go home on Saturday morning if we can take him via air ambulance."

"No problem," Nick said, cradling the receiver between his head and shoulder as he propped Dexter against his shoulder. "I'll arrange everything. Are you going to need a doctor on the flight?"

"We've got one here who's willing to come back with us—she's got leave and is headed stateside to see her mom and dad—if she can hitch a ride on our jet."

"I'll make sure that's okay when I make the arrangements for you," Nick said, aware he wasn't as happy as he would have expected to find his babysitting gig ending so soon. Probably because it meant he would no longer be sharing quarters with Amy. "How are you holding up?" he asked his little sister. He knew from personal experience how difficult situations like this were. Often, the period afterward was almost worse than the actual trauma.

"I'm pretty good," Lola said wearily. "I'm tired, but I guess that's to be expected. Mostly, I'm just relieved that Chuck's going to be all right."

"Me, too," Nick said sincerely. He would have hated for his sister to go through the rest of her life without her husband.

Lola's voice caught. "I just couldn't bear it if anything happened to Chuck or Dexter, Nick."

"I know," Nick said quietly as he cuddled his nephew closer and felt Dexter snuggle happily against him in return.

"That doesn't mean I understand or accept why these things happen to us, though," Lola said, a mixture of bitterness and anger creeping into her voice. "It just…it doesn't seem fair."

"It isn't fair," Nick returned as he walked back out onto the porch and sat down in the rocking chair, Dexter still in his arms. "But that's life. Full of random events and messiness and a lot of outcomes that just plain don't make sense."

"As well as love and joy," Lola reminded him.

"That, too." Although, Nick acknowledged, *he* hadn't had much of either in recent years.

"Enough about me and my feelings, though," Lola cleared her throat and continued in a much stronger voice, "How is Dexter doing?" she asked, unable to mask her deep longing to be with her baby.

"Dex is doing fine," Nick was happy to report. "As long as he gets to feel some skin while he's taking his bottle. You probably better warn Chuck about that. His kid has one wicked grip." Nick grimaced again as Dexter tugged on his chest hair again.

"How's the frozen breast milk holding out?" Lola asked.

Nick worked to disengage Dexter's fist. "We have enough to last us until this evening, then it's commercial formula until you get back. But don't worry. Dexter's been darn cooperative so far. I have no reason to think he won't continue to be," Nick said confidently.

"That's good. But, Nick…about Amy. I know she acts as if she can handle anything, but inside…she's vulnerable."

Nick tensed as he shifted Dexter around so his back

was to Nick's front. "What's that supposed to mean?" he demanded crankily.

"It means," Lola spelled out plainly, "I talked to Amy on the phone yesterday and I got the feeling she might be developing a little crush on you."

A lot more than a simple crush if the way Amy had made love to him the night before had been any indication, Nick thought guiltily.

"Amy doesn't know your history," Lola continued worriedly.

*And she doesn't need to know,* Nick thought. *No woman in my life does.*

"I just don't want to see her get hurt," Lola concluded.

"You don't think I could get hurt, too?" Nick prodded in an effort to deflect the argument away from what he didn't want to discuss.

He could almost see his sister frowning on the other end of the line.

"You're not as idealistic as she is, Nick. And certainly not anywhere near as emotional or romantic. Amy, on the other hand, still believes in happily-ever-after," Lola said sternly. "And I and everyone close to her want her to have it."

## Chapter Ten

"So what do you think?" Amy asked Nick late that afternoon.

Nick looked around his Charleston office suite. The room where he planned to conduct business was everything a successful executive could want, pulled together in an amazing amount of time. But it wasn't him. Not at all.

"What's wrong?" Amy asked as she rolled the infant stroller a little closer.

"Nothing," Nick fibbed, turning his gaze to the tinted windows and the view of the Charleston skyline. He had promised himself he wouldn't hurt Amy. Criticizing work that she had obviously put her heart and soul into would do just that.

"Like heck there isn't." Amy scowled at him. She strode closer, hands on her hips. "I've obviously done something wrong here," she said. "And I want to know what it is."

Nick wished she didn't look so beautiful in the

figure-hugging yellow sheath, white linen jacket and wedge-heeled sandals. Her soft and silky hair was held away from her face with a tortoiseshell clip. Her face was glowing with color. She looked both stunning and sure of herself, every inch the professional businesswoman and talented interior designer. And she'd gone to all this trouble for him.

"One professional to another, you owe me the truth," Amy continued with increasing determination as she looked him in the eye. "Because unless I know what's wrong in plain and simple terms, there's no way I can fix it for you, Nick," she warned, her soft voice sending shivers over his skin. "And if I don't fix it, I haven't pleased you—the client—and that means I haven't done my job." Amy paused, the hurt she felt on a personal level flickering momentarily in her turquoise eyes before disappearing completely. "I always do my job, Nick. I don't walk away until the customer is one hundred percent satisfied."

The only way Nick would feel satisfied again was if he was afforded the opportunity to make love with Amy again. But having already decided for both their sakes that that was not going to happen again, Nick pushed the unwelcome desire aside. He narrowed his eyes at Amy, determined to treat her, not like a one-time-lover of his, but like the professional decorator she was. "It's too warm and cozy," he stated simply. Too Southern in style. He wouldn't be able to be in a luxuriously comfortable environment like this without thinking of Amy.

Her eyes widened in surprise. "You don't like the soft leather furniture?" she asked, indicating the grouping in front of his desk.

Nick lifted his broad shoulders in a careless shrug. "It looks more suitable for taking a nap on." *Or making love to a woman,* he thought with increasing discomfort. But not just any woman. Only one woman. Amy. And Amy was the one woman he couldn't afford to get emotionally involved with.

"You had in mind something so stiffly uncomfortable no one would stay for long?" Amy quipped.

Nick wouldn't have put it like that. But her assessment, he realized, was right on the mark. Again. "Right." He liked to do business and get out, before the meetings turned to more personal, intimate subjects.

"And the desk?" Amy stepped closer in a drift of apple-blossom perfume.

"Too bulky," Nick decreed. When what he really meant was that the mahogany desk, with its rich glossy sheen, was too close to the color of Amy's hair. And he didn't want to be thinking of Amy every time he sat down behind it. No, he wanted to put Amy out of his mind and his heart as soon as this mutual baby-sitting job of theirs was over.

Otherwise...

Otherwise, they'd probably both end up getting hurt.

"What about the art on the walls?" Amy asked,

looking more puzzled than hurt now. As if she was trying to figure him out again.

Nick turned his attention to the framed paintings. The landscapes and seascapes were beautiful enough to get lost in. "Too intriguing. Maybe we should go with something more mundane."

"Let's move on to the next room." Her face expressionless, Amy crossed to the private quarters beyond. Once again, Nick found fault with practically everything. Not because, as he actually told her, the interior she had designed wasn't right for him, but because the private living quarters were so clearly to his taste, right down to the very last detail. No other decorator had ever been able to do that for him. For reasons he didn't quite understand, Nick didn't want Amy doing that for him now. Especially in what would be his bedroom.

"So basically I should just start over," Amy said matter-of-factly, when they had concluded their inventory. "And go for something cold and utilitarian and as impersonal as possible."

Exactly, Nick thought. He wanted the kind of office that revealed nothing about him, the kind that could belong to literally anyone. Out loud, though, he brushed off her attempts to please him and said, "Look, Amy, I don't see any reason to redo it—I'm not going to be here all that much, anyway. It's fine. What do I owe you?"

"At the moment, absolutely nothing because I

never accept payment until the customer is completely satisfied."

Nick blocked her way. "I'm never going to be completely satisfied with the decor, Amy."

"I know," she returned, her determination to succeed where others had failed before her evident. "But I'm going to keep trying, anyway."

IT DID NOT SURPRISE Nick that the mood between him and Amy was tense as they parted, with Amy taking charge of Dexter, while he went on to meet with Amy's mother and her mother's New York attorney. In fact, given his plans for the future, which did not include this tenderhearted woman, he should have been elated by the new bristliness in Amy's regard for him. He had been alone long enough to know that tension and unhappiness with each other could go a long way toward keeping Amy and him apart physically. And that was what he wanted, wasn't it? To keep the two of them from getting any closer and keep Amy from cooking up any more dreams of how his life should be run.

"We should definitely celebrate this," Grace said as soon as the preliminary papers had been signed detailing her intent to do a pilot show for Nick's production company.

Nick knew he'd be in the soup if he didn't show up by seven-thirty that evening, as promised, to take his shift with Dexter and help get some sort of meal together for the two of them, as well. On the other hand, this was a major coup. And if his new star wanted toasting...

"Whatever you like," Nick said, "you got it."

Grace smiled as she bid adieu to her attorney. "Then I'd like to have dinner with my daughter and you, Nick. And maybe take a turn holding that adorable nephew of yours, too."

*Not what he'd been prepared for,* Nick thought uneasily. But always one to roll with the punches, he smiled. "Just let me call Amy and tell her we're on our way."

Unfortunately Lola's phone went unanswered and Amy wasn't picking up her cell. So Nick had no way of forewarning Amy. He was just going to have to show up, her mother—and dinner for three—in tow.

"AREN'T YOU GOING to answer that?" Daisy asked when the telephone rang for what seemed like the twentieth time in as many minutes.

Amy looked at the caller ID box on Lola's portable phone and did her best to keep her emotions in check. Which was, after all, Amy reminded herself sternly, exactly what Nick wanted from her.

Amy looked back at Daisy, who was dressed in a pair of snug, low-slung jeans and a fashionable tank top that revealed a lot of trim tan midriff, both above and below her navel. Her pale blond hair was caught in a messy braid, and she wore big gold hoops in her ears that practically screamed free spirit. All in all an outfit that was not exactly up to snuff for the rest of the exceedingly uptight Templeton family. Which was probably why Daisy had selected it, Amy knew. Amy shrugged offhandedly as the phone continued to ring. "It's just Nick, telling me he's not going to be home for dinner this evening."

"How do you know that?" Daisy asked when the ringing finally stopped.

Amy juggled Dexter, who was holding a stuffed penguin in both chubby hands, on her knee. "Because Nick is meeting with my mother and her attorney and they've probably signed a deal, and my mother probably wants to go out on the town and celebrate."

"Hm." Daisy leaned forward and clasped her hands between her knees. "So why not pick up and let him tell you that?"

*Because I don't want to talk to him right now,* Amy thought stubbornly. "Because it's not that important and I'm trying to decide which of your photos I want to run in my newspaper ad this weekend," she said. She turned back to the photos spread across the coffee table in front of them. "I like the one of the Mc-Pherson bonus-room makeover," Amy said. "What do you think?"

Daisy turned a critical eye to both women's work. "I think any of your projects would get you more business, but yeah, I like that one. I think it has appeal to just about everyone. And it also shows how easily you incorporate elements for everyone in the family in one very pulled-together room."

Amy grinned at Daisy. "I think I should have you doing my advertising for me."

Daisy beamed. "You flatter me."

"I tell the truth," Amy corrected seriously. "How are things going with you?"

"Not good." Daisy sighed heavily. "I got kicked out of my parents' home."

Amy's eyes widened in surprise. For all the fighting between Daisy and her folks, there was no doubt—in Amy's mind, anyway—that Richard and Charlotte Templeton loved their daughter very much. They were just strict and overbearing in the way they demonstrated that love. But, having grown up there, Daisy had to be used to that. "Why?" Amy asked.

Legs stretched out in front of her, Daisy slid down and slouched against the back of the sofa. She turned her gaze to the beams on the cottage ceiling. "They're ticked off about my continuing search for my biological parents. They don't understand why I want to find them. Anyway—" Daisy sat upright again "—the money I have been paying private detective Harlan Decker is seriously depleting my savings, and in an effort to further rein me in, my parents cut off my allowance and took away my car. So I had to go out and buy one on my own, which really emptied my bank account. And to make matters worse, I'm having trouble finding a place I can afford. All the landlords think it's great I'm a photographer by trade, but to be able to rent one of their apartments, I need to have a regular job with a regular paycheck.

Being a freelance photographer does not qualify me for that. At least not right now, anyway.''

"Can't you get your brother, Connor, to take you in?" He was not only a successful commercial real-estate broker, he was single. And, as far as Amy knew, romantically unattached.

"That's where I'm staying now—on his sofa—but that's not working out very well, either," Daisy admitted unhappily.

"Why not?" Loving the way the baby felt cuddled on her lap, Amy pressed a kiss to the top of Dexter's head.

Daisy made a face. "Because dear Connor has a tendency to either lecture me on the ill advisedness of my ways or overprotect me. Neither of which I find very much fun."

Amy commiserated as Dexter bopped her on the arm with his stuffed animal. "I hear you. My brothers are the same way." And Amy had an idea what they would say if they knew she had thrown caution to the wind and gone ahead and slept with Nick the night before, despite all Deveraux advice to the contrary.

"Anyway, I'll figure it out eventually," Daisy concluded. She paused uncertainly, a hint of color coming into her cheeks. "In the meantime, I have something to ask you."

"Fire away."

"How well do you know Jack Granger?"

Amy hesitated, aware that she could call on Jack in an emergency requiring legal expertise or talk to him at a party, but other than that, she had never really spent any time with him. "Not all that well, I guess." Amy frowned. "Why?"

The color in Daisy's cheeks deepened. "He works for your father, doesn't he?"

Amy nodded. "He's chief legal counsel for Deveraux Shipping. Why?"

Daisy bit her lower lip and turned worried eyes to Amy. "I keep running into him, lately. And it doesn't really seem to be an accident."

That did not sound like the Jack Granger Amy knew. That Jack was all work and no play. He liked to run on the beach in his spare time or go sea kayaking with her brothers Chase and Gabe. He never went to any of the society functions, and as far as she knew, avoided the singles scene in Charleston, as well. Which made his showing up where the noticeably wild and fun-loving Daisy hung out all the odder. "You think he's hitting on you?"

Daisy fingered the end of her braid and smiled at Amy self-consciously. "More like nosing around in my business and trying to get chummy with me. Not that that makes any sense, either."

Amy wasn't so sure. "You are very pretty."

Daisy shook her head emphatically. "I don't think Jack's interested in that aspect of me."

Amy's eyes widened as Dexter kicked and cooed. "You think Jack is after you because he wants your money?" An heiress herself, Amy knew that feeling. She could usually spot the guys that wanted a rich wife miles away, and assumed Daisy, who was set to inherit a considerable fortune of her own, could, too.

"Nope."

"Then what?" Amy persisted, really curious now.

"That's just it." Daisy shrugged and got to her feet. She began to pace the living room restlessly. "I don't know. I just have a feeling all these chance meetings Jack Granger and I have been having are no accident."

"Well, I haven't got a clue why Jack would be chasing you," Amy said, perplexed. "But if I find out anything, I'll let you know."

"Thanks, Amy." Daisy smiled. "I'd appreciate that."

"In the meantime, maybe I can help you out financially by giving you more work. I've got five redecorating projects that need photographed. Interested?"

"Absolutely."

Amy checked her appointment book and wrote out the address, names and phone numbers. "The customers already agreed to this. You'll just have to set up the times that are convenient."

The door opened behind them. Nick walked in, Grace right behind him.

"Mom!" Amy stood up, surprised to see her mother coming in with Nick, take-out bags from the Magnolia Grill in hand.

"Hello, Amy. Daisy." Grace's voice was noticeably cooler on the second acknowledgment.

"Mrs. Deveraux." Daisy nodded at Grace, then began hastily gathering up her things.

"I don't think you've met Nick." Amy introduced the two.

Daisy beamed as she shook Nick's hand, then turned to Amy. "Well, listen. I've got to go."

"Sure you don't want to join us for dinner?" Amy asked, not in the least bit anxious to be alone with her mother and Nick. "From the looks of it—" she glanced at the take-out bags "—we've got plenty."

"No thanks." Daisy winked. "I've got a private detective to see. Ciao, you-all." With that she breezed out the door.

Amy wasn't surprised to see that Grace remained tense even after Daisy had left. She turned to her mother. "Why do you do that?" she asked, irritated.

"What?" Grace asked as if she didn't know.

"Behave so coolly toward her," Amy explained.

Grace's expression tightened defensively. "I don't think I do that."

Amy gave her mother a look. "Mom, you've never liked her. And for the life of me, I can't figure out why."

Abruptly, Grace looked tense and unhappy again. "She's an undisciplined troublemaker." Grace pushed the words through her teeth.

"She's never made any trouble for us," Amy protested, not understanding why her mother, usually one of the warmest and most gracious women around, would have such a closed mind when it came to Daisy.

"She's made plenty for others."

"For her family. And from what I've noted, you don't seem to like any of the Templetons any better than you like Daisy." Except for Connor and Iris—Daisy's much older, recently widowed sister—Amy didn't, either. But that was neither here nor there, when it came to Daisy.

"Can we not talk about this?" Grace asked in a disgruntled tone.

Infuriated that her mother was pulling the doors shut on her once again, refusing to tell Amy what was in her heart or on her mind in this very tricky situation, Amy figured that as long as they were going to argue, they might as well argue about something relevant to the two of them. She handed Dexter to Nick to hold and shot back sweetly, "What would you like me to talk about, then, Mother? My living arrangements here with Nick, of which you heartily disapprove? Or perhaps your most inappropriate relationship with Paulo?"

"Amy," Nick interrupted in a low, warning tone, as he stepped between the two women.

"My love life or lack thereof is none of your business, Amy," Grace said calmly, moving around Nick to square off with Amy.

"Which is probably as it should be," Amy said, doing nothing to conceal the hurt and frustration she felt at being so far apart emotionally from her mother once again. "The question is," she said, as she looked at Grace steadily, "is it any of Dad's?"

NO DOUBT ABOUT IT, Nick thought, Amy had just thrown down the gauntlet. And it looked as if her mother was going to be quick to pick it right back up. "Amy, I am not going to discuss this with you," Grace said calmly.

"Fine. Shut me out the way you've always shut Dad out." Her shoulders rigid with hurt pride, Amy turned away and headed for the back porch.

Oblivious to the fact that Nick and Dexter were there watching, Grace went after her daughter, cutting her off at the pass. She took Amy by the elbow and forced her daughter to look at her. "What did you just say?" she demanded angrily.

Tears glistening in her eyes, Amy retorted emotionally, "I'm saying I know that Dad begged you to try and work things out and give the two of you another chance, and you wouldn't give him the time of day!" The color left Grace's face so quickly Nick thought she might faint. Before he could get to her, Amy was there, holding her mother by both arms.

"He loved you, Mom. He *still* loves you, and you just won't let him anywhere near you!"

Grace's chin set stubbornly. Her voice reverberated with hurt. "It's a complicated situation, Amy."

Amy glared at her mother. "You could make it simple if you wanted."

Grace sighed, looking so shaky Nick's heart went out to her.

Figuring enough was enough, Nick settled Dexter in his baby swing and then moved to intervene. "Amy," Nick said sternly. "How about not doing this anymore?"

"Fine with me," Amy snapped.

"Fine with me, too," Grace said wearily.

"Now, about dinner…" Nick said, still feeling as if he'd stepped into the center of a heavy weight fight.

"I've lost my appetite," Grace said, looking around for her handbag. When she found it, she picked it up and said, "I think I'll just go home."

"I'll drive you," Nick offered, casting Amy another censuring look.

"No." Grace held up a staying hand. "I'll take a cab."

"I insist," Nick said. He turned to Amy again. "You and I will talk when I get back," he promised.

Amy released a frustrated breath. She did not appear to be looking forward to it.

WHEN NICK LET himself into the cottage, Amy was on the phone. She shot him a withering glance, then turned her back to him and continued her conversation. "It sounds wonderful, Aunt Winnifred. Of course I'd be delighted to come to a welcome-to-the-family party for Eleanor Saturday evening. Nick? Well, I guess he could come. I'll ask him. But he might be busy."

Nick went into the nursery to check on Dexter, who was sound asleep in his crib, and then came back out to the living room.

Amy was still talking on the phone. "I have no control over that, Aunt Winnifred. No. No, you and Great-Aunt Eleanor don't need to make any phone calls. I'll deliver the invitation to Nick myself. I promise. Okay. Goodbye." She hung up, then turned to face him and reported both dutifully and reluctantly, "There's a family party for my long-lost aunt on Saturday evening. You're invited."

Nick lifted his brow and asked, "As your date?"

A faint blush tinged Amy's cheeks. "I imagine that's Eleanor and Winnifred's intention—they can't seem to stop themselves from matchmaking—but you're welcome to go alone or even with my mother if you like." Amy gritted her teeth, some of her earlier angst coming to the fore once again as she turned her glance away from Nick's boldly assessing gaze. "Who knows? Maybe that would stop her from showing up on Paulo's arm."

Nick followed Amy into the kitchen. "Who is this Paulo you're talking about?" And why was Amy, who had just chastised her own mother for being close-minded about Daisy Templeton, so opposed to him?

"Paulo is a young and very virile-looking yoga instructor," Amy said, making no effort to hide her disapproval as she opened the refrigerator door.

"He's half my mother's age and has hair down to his shoulders."

Able to at least partially understand Amy's dislike of the man, Nick set the oven thermostat and then concluded, "The antithesis of your buttoned-up CEO-father, in other words."

Her turquoise eyes wary, Amy watched as Nick took off his suit jacket and tie, then hung both over the back of a chair. She folded her arms. "Something like that."

Wanting to get at least half as comfortable as Amy, who was wearing her usual after-work shorts and shirt, Nick unbuttoned the first two buttons on his shirt and rolled up his sleeves. "Doesn't really sound like your mother's type," he noted casually, trying not to notice how slender and sexy her bare legs were, how cute her bare feet and red toenails.

Amy's lower lip slid out in a delicious pout. "What's your point?"

Nick took off the cardboard covers and put the entrées from the Magnolia Grill in the oven to warm, as per the directions on the foil containers. Finished, he turned back to Amy, ready to say his piece. "Maybe your mother is only dating this Paulo because she knows she could never really get serious about him."

Amy blinked. "I hadn't thought of it that way," she said slowly after a moment, looking a little less ready to do battle.

"Maybe you should," Nick advised gently but

firmly. Moving around Amy, he got out the plates, silverware and glasses, and set them on the table. "And by the way, you owe your mother an apology," he continued, doing his best to do what he could to mend the rift between mother and daughter. "You were awfully rough on her." He had told Grace the same on the drive back to her rented residence.

"I'm sorry you saw it," Amy retorted stonily as she opened the container of salad and put that on the table, too. She squared her shoulders defiantly, the motion lifting her breasts. "I'm not sorry I said what I did." Amy glared at Nick resentfully as she confided, "The truth is I should have said it a long time ago, instead of keeping it all bottled up inside."

Nick knew Amy hated that her parents had divorced and wanted them back together. But that didn't make it possible, or even probable. And it was high time Amy realized that. He held Amy's chair for her, watched as she slid into it, then said sternly, "It takes two to make—or break—a marriage, Amy."

Fire flashed in her eyes. "How do you know?" she demanded resentfully as Nick settled opposite her.

"Because," Nick said simply, "I've been there."

## Chapter Eleven

Amy stared at Nick, aware this was the first time he had talked to her about something so intimate, aware they were finally getting somewhere, talking about the things that would enable them to get closer. She asked gently, "What do you mean, you've been there?"

Appearing as if this was very hard for him to discuss, Nick forked up some salad. "I mean I've been married," he said grimly as his face took on a brooding, faraway look. "And it ended badly. We were both to blame. And I'll probably never forgive myself for what happened, but that doesn't mean I run around discussing it or wearing a hair shirt to punish myself. And neither," Nick said heavily, "should your mother."

Amy ignored his defense of her mother and concentrated on the empathy in his low tone. "So what happened to your wife?"

Nick's shoulders tensed beneath the starched fabric of his olive-green dress shirt. He released a weary sigh and his gaze collided with Amy's once again. "She died." Nick swallowed, looking as if he wished he had never started this conversation.

Amy could only imagine the horror of losing a spouse. Her heart going out to him, she touched the back of his wrist with her hand and asked gently, "How?" And when?

Nick sat back in his chair. "In a fire at our home."

Aware his skin was warm—too warm—beneath her fingertips, Amy withdrew her hand and sat back, too. "Were you there?" she asked quietly, aware he bore no physical scars of the event.

"No." Nick looked as if that had made it even worse.

"Which is why it's your fault." Amy guessed his feelings as she studied him. Along with Nick's hurt was resignation and some degree of lingering consternation. She knew all about the guilt and second-guessing of past events, for she had suffered the same when her relationship with Kirk had ended. She'd wondered if there was something she could have done differently to prevent what had happened, if there was something she should have seen or predicted that would have changed everything, and her heart told her that Nick was feeling the same way.

Nick shoved a hand through his hair. He got up and went to the oven to check on the food. Finding it in need of more time, he returned to the table and sat down restlessly. "It's my fault because I knew the furnace hadn't been inspected yet that year, and I was lax about calling to get it done because I was busy working two jobs to pay for the place and the baby we were going to have in another six months.''

Oh, my God, Amy thought, shaken. He had not only lost a wife, but an unborn child in one incredible tragedy.

''Had I done that, had I been there that evening,'' Nick continued in a voice that was firm with resolve, ''I never would have let my wife turn the damned heater on right before she went to bed that night. We would have gone to a motel, instead, if that was what we had to do to keep her and the baby she was carrying warm, rather than risk turning on a gas furnace that hadn't been inspected.''

Nick swallowed and looked more tortured and remote. ''Instead,'' he continued in a voice laced with pain and self-recrimination as he turned his eyes back to hers, ''I didn't give either the furnace or my wife and baby's safety a moment's thought until someone from the fire department showed up to tell me what had happened.''

Amy reached out to touch him again, wordlessly comforting him.

''The point is, Amy, it was my fault,'' he told her as he continued to look at her with dark, brooding eyes. ''And I have a million regrets and more guilt for the way things turned out than I will ever be able to deal with, as does, I suspect, your mother. But there's nothing that can be done about what happened to my wife and unborn child,'' he said hoarsely.

"Any more than there is anything that can be done about what happened between your parents years ago."

"Except," Amy qualified, wanting Nick to see the distinction, just as she did, "my parents still have a chance to get back together again."

Nick paused, weighing what she said as he continued to grip her hands tightly, then said quietly. "If they do reconcile, it should be up to them, not because anyone in their family—even their kids, even you— is pushing them to do it, Amy."

She was silent, considering his advice. Able to tell from the aromas coming from the oven that their dinner was ready, she stood. "I can't help it." Amy grabbed the oven mitts and went to the oven. "I want my family intact," she said as she took their piping-hot dinners from the oven, carried them to the table and set them down, at both places. "And I know my parents still love each other."

"What if it still doesn't work?" Nick got up to get the salt and pepper from the spice rack on the counter. He carried them back to the table.

"Then at least I'll know I tried," Amy said. That was better than standing by and doing nothing. Silence fell between them as they stood facing each other. Amy could tell Nick still didn't approve of what she was doing. But she no longer cared so much about that. What mattered to her was that he had confided in her. Her heart aching for what he had been through, even as her hopes rose for their future, Amy closed the distance between them and put her arms around his waist. "I'm sorry about your loss, Nick," she said softly, tenderly.

Nick grimaced, released a beleaguered breath and looked at her as if she was a fool for wanting him. "I don't want your pity, Amy," he told her stoically.

"Then how about," she countered just as emphatically, refusing to let him wall himself off now that he had begun to let her close, "my love and tenderness?"

KNOWING HE HAD TO PROTECT Amy from getting even more hurt than she was already bound to be, given that he had been foolish enough to succumb to temptation and make love with her, Nick placed his hands on her shoulders and moved her away from him. She deserved and would someday get so much more than what he had to offer. He looked at her steadily. "You don't love me." And if he had his way, she never would.

Amy merely smiled, more tranquil than ever. "I could if you would let me," she said.

Nick swallowed around the lump in his throat. "I'm not cut out for marriage, Amy." How miserably he had proved that.

"I don't know how you can say that," she said.

"I say that," Nick told her brusquely, the grief and guilt welling up inside him to a disabling degree as he looked deep into her eye, "because I've already done a lousy job of protecting my wife and child once, and I'm not going to do it again." And he sure as hell wasn't going to do it to Amy and any child she might have.

"So do a better job," Amy advised seriously. "And expect your wife to do a better job, too, because whether you want to admit it or not, Nick, this was equally her fault. She should have known better. Acted more wisely. Protected herself and your child."

Part of Nick knew that what Amy said was true. The other part felt he should have been able to circumvent what had eventually happened. Only knowing for certain that he wanted the pain of remembering to stop, he drew a ragged breath and said, "I'm going to go one step further than that. I'm going to opt out of the possibility of hurting anyone ever again. That's why I don't get emotionally involved with women."

She lifted a delicate brow. "You tell them all this?"

"No." Once again, he avoided her eyes.

"Just your rules," she guessed.

Nick ran his hand over his face as if that would take away some of the sorrow from his heart. "Right," he admitted as impassively as he could.

"Then why me?" Amy persisted, once more reading a lot more into his actions than he wanted.

"I don't know," Nick replied gruffly. The truth was, he was already beginning to regret it, because he could already see the romantic in Amy making this into some sort of soap-opera problem just waiting to be solved. And it wasn't that way at all. Nick had had years to figure out he was never going to recover from the devastating loss. Never going to let anyone else down that way again. Never going to open himself up to that kind of hurt.

Amy glided closer in a drift of apple blossom. "Well, I do know why you told me. You told me because you want to be close to me."

Wanting and doing were two different things. How well Nick knew that. And although he might not have been as smart as he should have been before about the women in his life, he was wiser now. And a lot more disciplined. "I told you," he explained to Amy with a matter-of-factness he couldn't begin to feel, "so you'd stop having impossibly unrealistic thoughts about where this whatever-it-is-between-us might lead." *I told you so you'd stop thinking I was going to be the one who would make all your dreams come true and enable you to live happily ever after.* Nick wanted Amy to be as realistic in her thinking as he was being—even if it hurt.

Amy studied him for a long moment. "Okay," she said, backing off abruptly. "If that's the way you want it—" she regarded him with icy disdain "—that's the way it will be."

NICK HAD THOUGHT he knew what loneliness was. But he soon realized that he hadn't a clue until now. It shouldn't have mattered to him that Amy took her dinner and finished it out on the porch between phone calls to various suppliers and clients. It shouldn't have mattered that she went to bed as soon as she had finished, or that once again he had the sofa and the rest of the cottage to himself. But somehow it did.

For the first time in years, he was unable to keep his mind on his work. Television didn't interest him. Nor did Lola's collection of DVD movies or books. With Dexter still asleep and Amy in bed for the night, he finally decided the best thing to do was to go out for a midnight run. So he changed into shorts and a T-shirt and slipped outside. The moon was full, the night sky clear. Nick stretched and then took off down the lonely country road.

Six miles later he was back at the foot of the lane to the cottage, feeling no less stressed about the situation, but a lot more physically relaxed. And that was when he heard it—Dexter screaming at the top of his lungs. Nick raced down the lane, up onto the porch and, after pausing to unlock the door, into the cottage. Amy was in the living area, a loudly bawling Dexter in her arms. "What happened?" Nick panted, as he reached for the squalling, thrashing infant.

Amy shoved the sleep-tousled hair from her eyes. Her cheeks were pink, her eyes still sleepy. She was clad in nothing but a sheer nightgown. As he felt his body immediately respond to the sight, he thought that she definitely should have put on a robe. "We're officially out of Lola's breast milk and he doesn't like the formula you bought at the store," Amy reported.

"Did you try the soy?"

"No."

Amy led the way back into the kitchen. Nick followed, holding Dexter away from his own sweaty body. "Let's try the soy."

"Okay."

Nick stripped off his damp T-shirt while Amy held Dexter and tossed a clean dish towel over his bare shoulder and chest. Thinking it might help divert his ticked-off nephew, Nick turned Dexter so he could watch Amy, too. Anchoring his right arm around Dexter's middle, Nick held Dexter with Dexter's back to his chest, his bottom perched on his left forearm.

Dexter's squalls subsided as Amy quickly fixed a bottle of the formula. She warmed it gently in the microwave, shook it well, tested it and handed it over to Nick. Nick leaned against the counter and offered it to Dexter. Dexter took one taste and spit it out. His face turned beet-red and he let out another heart-wrenching wail.

"Maybe the third time is the charm," Nick said, handing Dexter back to Amy and fixing a fourth bottle of the last kind of formula they had on hand to try. To his and Amy's mutual dismay, Dexter reacted just as unhappily to this iron-fortified kind as he had to all the rest. "It's just not his mother's milk," Amy said, pacing back and forth as an upset Dexter continued to vent his feelings in her arms.

"There must be some way to make him like this," Nick said anxiously. Just as there had to be some way for him to stop responding to the sight of Amy in her nightgown. After all, it wasn't the first time he had seen her looking so breathtakingly beautiful or in her nightclothes. After days under the same roof, he ought to be used to both by now!

"I don't know how," Amy muttered, as she studied the discarded baby bottles with a perplexed frown, "unless we put chocolate syrup in it."

Nick's spirits rose at the brilliance of that statement. He took Dexter back from Amy. "Call your brother Gabe. Ask him if there's a reason, medically speaking, why we can't do that."

Amy flushed even as she picked up the phone and began to dial. "I'm sure it's against all established guidelines."

"Only one way to find out," Nick said, confident Gabe Deveraux would help them find the solution.

Seconds later Amy had her doctor-brother on the line. A short conversation followed. Finished, she hung up and turned back to Nick, her eyes alight. "Gabe said a touch of chocolate probably wouldn't hurt him, but the caffeine in it could keep him awake."

Nick was already looking in the refrigerator for other possibilities. He shot a look over his shoulder as the first possibility surfaced. "Strawberry syrup?"

Amy bit her lip and edged closer. "Gabe said that might cause an allergic reaction. And honey and corn syrup are something babies shouldn't have—both can cause botulism in infants. But he said we *could* try a tiny bit of granulated white sugar, just for tonight.

Then tomorrow try adding just a touch of baby food peaches or applesauce to the formula to sweeten it and disguise the taste. But just until Lola gets back on Saturday. Then it's back to the norm.''

"Works for me. Now if it just works for him." Nick waited for Amy to add a little sugar to Dexter's bottle, and then he offered it to the infant. Dexter screwed up his face as he sucked gingerly on the nipple, then his features began to relax and he began sucking in earnest.

Nick grinned at Amy. "Score one for our team," he murmured victoriously.

Amy smiled back at Nick and continued holding Dexter close to her as he sucked eagerly on the bottle. She sank onto the rocking chair in the living room, looking very beautiful, maternal and disheveled. Knowing if he didn't do something soon, he *would* end up making love to her again, Nick turned away. Aware he was still hot and sweaty, he asked, "Mind if I shower while you're doing that?''

"Go ahead," Amy said, her attention fixed solely on Dexter. Heart pounding, body aching, Nick slipped into the bathroom.

THE SHOWER RAN for a very long time. So long, in fact, Amy figured they were probably close to being completely out of hot water. But that was okay, she thought as she picked up a sleeping Dexter, carried him gently into the bedroom and lowered him into the crib. His back had barely hit the mattress when the bathroom door eased open. Steam wafted out. Nick followed, clad only in a towel. Walking softly, he passed her and headed out into the living room, where his suitcase sat open on the floor. "Forgot to take clean clothes in with me," he said.

Her heart racing, Amy lounged in the portal. She loved the way he looked, all hard muscle and smooth skin, his chest sprinkled with whorls of curling brown hair. The towel rode low, exposing the flatness of his abdomen and burgeoning arousal. "I like you just the way you are." *I like you wanting me,* Amy thought. And there's no denying you want me. Very much.

Nick's eyes darkened. "Amy…" he warned huskily as she gracefully and resolutely closed the distance between them, not stopping until they were toe-to-toe.

Amy tucked her hands in the edge of his towel, pulling him closer. She wasn't going to let the best thing that had ever happened to her go without a fight. She tipped her head back and regarded him steadily. "We can't pretend what happened last night didn't happen, Nick."

He rested his hands on her shoulders, the warmth of his palms burning his skin. "You're not cut out for a short-term love affair."

It wouldn't be short-term if he gave them half a chance, Amy thought. But not wanting to push too hard, too fast, she merely went up on tiptoe and laced her hands around his neck. She fit her lips to his, the happiness she felt when she was with him flooding through her. "Wrong, Nick. This is exactly what I'm cut out for."

Nick told himself he wasn't going to kiss her. Wasn't going to let the passion get the best of him this time. But the moment her soft mouth pressed his, he was as lost as he'd been the first time. And just as vulnerable to her and the love she was offering so selflessly. With a groan, Nick wrapped his arms around her and brought her against him. Delighting in the fragrant smell of her, the loving way she fit her body against him, he kissed her long and hard and deep. He kissed her until they were both trembling, and then, unable to wait any longer, he swept her up into his arms and carried her into the bedroom, where he set her down on the rumpled covers of her bed.

Her eyes widened as he let the towel fall, helped her off with her gown and joined her on the bed. Lying on his side, he took her in his arms again. Cushioning her head and neck with one arm, he kissed her with slow, insistent demand, knowing neither of them would be satisfied until he made her his again. When he cupped her breast, she trembled with pleasure and moved her hips against his insistently, in the same rhythm as his tongue in her mouth.

The blood thundered through him, pooling low, and he reveled in the soft surrender of her body against his. Knowing he wouldn't last much longer, he pressed his sex into the cradle of her legs, and then, holding off his own pleasure, shifted her so she was on her back and placed a pillow beneath her hips.

"Nick..." Her lips were set and swollen from their kisses. Her eyes glowed. Her body was flushed and waiting. Nick knew he hadn't done anything to deserve Amy's love. And even though he couldn't give her what she wanted in return, he knew he could give her a night of pleasure she would never forget.

Amy trembled as Nick kissed her thoroughly once again and then slid down to the triangle between her legs. She arched her back and caught his head between her hands. Her eyes drifted shut and she sighed as his lips found her center. The tenderness of his lovemaking nearly her undoing, she arched and came apart in hot, aching waves. And still he wasn't finished. He cradled her between his hands, stroking her repeatedly, until she was unable to bear it, until she was calling out his name, and then he was sliding up and over her once again, moving to possess her in one smooth thrust, taking everything she offered, giving her everything in return. Gasping in pleasure, she wrapped her arms and legs around him, holding him close, bringing him deeper yet.

And then they shifted again, Nick on his back, Amy draped over him. Moving up, gliding up over the length of the rigid length of him, making him moan. Replacing her body with her lips and tongue, she loved him as he had loved her. Driving him to the point of madness until he had her where he wanted her again and he was deep inside her. Their mouths mated, just as their bodies did, in one hot delicious kiss, and then they were moving together, demanding everything each other had to give, pleasing, daring, wanting, until for the first time Amy knew what it was like to really love someone without restraint.

And Nick discovered it, too. He had never wanted a woman to be his the way he wanted Amy. Never felt so completely a part of another. And even though he knew it couldn't last, he held on to the moment—and to her—with every shred of his being. Taking her until she was shuddering in frissons of endless pleasure and so was he. Until reality spun away and they were locked in a bliss unlike anything he had ever known.

To AMY'S DELIGHT, they made love again and again, finally falling asleep around three-thirty wrapped in each other's arms. She expected to wake that way, too. But to her disappointment, it didn't happen. When she stirred again, it was almost six o'clock. She was alone in the bed.

She threw on her robe and glanced into the living room. Nick was there, sitting at the desk. Dexter was sitting on Nick's lap, looking cozy as could be, while Nick worked on his laptop computer. Amy didn't need to talk to him to see the way it was going to be. She could tell by his excessively businesslike demeanor, the fact he was already dressed and up, the coffee made, that he was going to behave as if their night together was already a thing of the past.

Doing her best to disguise her hurt, Amy drew her

robe closer around her, and ventured over to stand beside them. "You're getting an early start," she observed.

Nick shot her a cursory smile that effectively negated the closeness they had shared during the night. "I've been neglecting my business," he told her calmly but pleasantly, before turning away once again. "I don't think I even looked at my e-mail yesterday and I know I didn't check my phone messages."

Amy put her hand in front of the computer screen. Nick looked up at her inquiringly. She knew what he felt—that because of his past mistakes he didn't deserve a future. Just as she knew he was wrong. "Is this the way it's going to be?" she asked quietly, aware once again she was wearing her heart on her sleeve and that it was his for the taking. And that she didn't care how long it took or what she had to do, if only he would love her back with even a smidgen of the intensity of what she was feeling for him.

Nick paused, his armor up, expression wary. "What do you mean?"

Amy plucked Dexter from Nick's lap, sat where the baby had been and turned loving eyes to Nick. "I'm talking about you—running away from me, from us, every time we make love," she explained gently.

In that instant Nick looked more vulnerable than Amy had ever seen him. "I told you I'm not a hearts-and-flowers kind of guy, Amy," he said. "I told you how I feel—that I'm not going to pretend to offer you the kind of future you want and need or be there to see the dawn with you.''

But he had made love to her again and again, Amy thought, the eternal optimist in her insisting that Nick was already changing, even if he was reluctant to admit it just yet.

She studied his face. She knew he was spoiling for a fight, and she thought she just might give it to him, if only to clear the air and make each other's feelings known in a way he might not otherwise do. ''And what am I supposed to say to that? That our being together last night was a mistake?'' Amy asked quietly.

Nick paused a moment. ''That's usually the female reaction,'' he conceded.

''Well, I don't think it was a mistake,'' Amy retorted firmly, knowing she had to find some way to get Nick to stop living out the heartache of the past on a daily basis and start thinking about his future. Their future. Perhaps some straight talk would do it. ''I think, Nick Everton, that I am the best thing that ever happened to you,'' she told him confidently. ''And one day soon you will realize it, too.'' She stood, handed Dexter back to him and slipped out of the room as softly and unobtrusively as she had come into it.

# Chapter Twelve

"Careful, guys," Amy said as the movers picked up the last of the furniture in Nick's office. "We want a full return on this stuff—that won't happen if any of it is scratched." She watched as the movers carried Nick's sofa out the door.

No sooner had they disappeared down the hall than Grace Deveraux stepped in.

No doubt about it, Amy thought, as she regarded her mother in the sunlight streaming in through the tinted floor-to-ceiling windows, her mother was looking a lot happier these days. Rested, relaxed, enthused about her future. That hadn't been the case when Grace had come to Charleston several months before after being fired from her job. Then she had been stressed and vulnerable and worried.

Amy had expected her mom to turn to her father under those circumstances, and briefly, Grace had. But as always, her parents' relationship had fallen apart in no time flat. For reasons Amy probably never would understand.

"What's going on here?" Grace asked, her expression perplexed as she watched Amy direct the movers with the expertise of a pro. "I thought Nick asked you to decorate his office, not clear it out."

"I did decorate it." Amy took the plant out of the corner and set it next to the door. "He just didn't like what I did. I think it was too homey and comfortable." Which was, in itself, a bad sign. "He wanted something sleeker and more sophisticated for his office here."

"It's not like you to get it wrong," Grace mused. She eyed Amy thoughtfully. "Usually you're an ace at summing up what people want and need in their homes."

Amy sighed and shoved a hand through her hair. "Well, with Nick I was way off the mark," she admitted with weary candor. "About that, anyway." Amy did not think she was wrong about what Nick needed and wanted in his life. The problem was getting Nick to admit he needed both physical and emotional comfort, love and intimacy.

Grace put down her purse and briefcase on the window ledge and looked into the second room, which had also been emptied out. Seeing that she and Amy were quite alone, Grace went back and closed the office door, ensuring their privacy. "As long as we have a minute…" Grace said.

At the look on her mother's face, it was all Amy could do not to groan. "If you're going to lecture me—"

"Not lecture," Grace said. "Offer advice."

Amy folded her arms. "Same thing."

"No, Amy, it's not. Look, I know you're too old to be getting advice from me about a man...."

Amy gritted her teeth. "Yes, Mom, I am."

"Nevertheless," Grace continued, "I feel I must warn you about Nick. As much as I admire his business acumen, I want to make sure you don't get yourself in another no-win situation here, Amy. Nick Everton is a devout bachelor, by reputation. It's not widely known, but he was married once, years ago, and he vowed that after he lost his wife, he would never marry again. He's kept that vow, honey. Because since then no woman has ever stayed in Nick's life for long."

A trickle of unease slid across Amy's shoulders, but she forced herself to remain confident and calm. "That could change, Mom."

Grace's eyes glowed with concern. "And what if it doesn't?" she queried softly, looking Amy straight in the eye. "Has Nick indicated to you that he is now looking for something more? Or are you just hoping that he'll do an about-face? Because I have to tell you, people don't change, especially not after so many years of living one's life a certain way."

*Leave it to her mother to make her feel like a hopeless idiot.* Before Amy could stop herself, she was blurting out what was on her mind and in her heart. "Well, if anyone should know about that, it's you and Dad." Then, seeing the hurt look on her mother's face and realizing how uncaring and childish her retort had sounded, immediately regretted the remark. "I'm sorry, Mom." Amy struggled to combat the flush of humiliation creeping from her neck into her face. She wished she could turn back the clock and erase that comment. But it was impossible. She had hurt her mother, even more than her mother had hurt her.

Amy swallowed hard and did her best to repair the damage. "I don't know what gets into me sometimes." She gestured ineffectually. "I'm able to be mature about everything and everyone else. But when it comes to you and Dad and the divorce..."

"It still hurts," Grace guessed gently.

Without warning, Amy's eyes were swimming with tears. She shook her head and fought to keep from crying. "Stupid, isn't it?" she agreed self-effacingly. "That I can't get over this."

A mixture of sadness and acceptance in her eyes, Grace closed the distance between them and gently touched Amy's shoulder. "The truth is, honey, none of us can. Divorce is one of those gifts that just keeps on giving. And giving and giving and giving."

Amy smiled through her tears at the truth in her mother's wry observation.

Grace guided Amy over to sit with her on the window ledge. "And you were still living at home with us when it happened—just fifteen. Your brothers were older, more independent than you were then, and because of that, I think our separation and eventual divorce didn't hit them as hard as it hit you."

"It's no excuse for my juvenile behavior now," Amy said as she brushed the tears away with her fingers. She shook her head in self-remonstration. "I shouldn't have said what I just did."

"Apology accepted," Grace said briskly, already moving on, as was her habit, leaving the family strife of the past behind her. "But back to Nick."

Amy groaned at her mother's unstoppable nature.

"I admire the way he has put himself out for his sister and her family, Amy. I respect what he can do in business, and appreciate what he wants to do for me. But the fact that deep down, Nick is a very good and decent and smart man," Grace said, "does not make him ready or open to love."

Aware her mother wouldn't be saying this if she didn't believe it with all her heart, Amy swallowed hard around the growing tension in her throat. "You're saying I could get hurt here."

Grace nodded. "More hurt than you have ever been. So be careful, honey. *Be very careful.*"

"HARD TO BELIEVE, isn't it?" Nick told Dexter as he sat with the baby in the rocker on the back porch while they were waiting for Amy to get dressed. "Your mommy is finally coming home—and she's bringing your daddy. The two of you will get to meet for the first time, and I can only imagine how proud and happy he is going to be to finally see, up close and personal, what a fine son he has."

Dexter gurgled and waved his arms and legs.

"Of course it's not all good news," Nick said, sighing. "It also means you and I won't be seeing nearly as much of each other as we have been." And Nick was going to miss that. He'd thought he didn't want kids. He was beginning to see he might be wrong about that. Even though wanting a child and being able to properly protect and care for a child over the long haul were two different things.

Nick cuddled Dexter closer. "Nor will we be seeing as much of Amy."

*Which was yet another reason to feel blue.* She had irritated him immensely in the beginning, as she tried to bring him all the way back to life. Tried to make him want what he had given up wanting. Now, even though Nick had never agreed with what Amy had tried to do, it was going to be hard not having her around twenty-four hours a day, seven days a week. He'd grown accustomed to being with her and meshing schedules with her, and even caring for Dexter with her. The three of them had felt like an instant family. He was surprised to realize he didn't want to give that up.

Dexter regarded Nick expectantly. "'Cause I've got my own life to go back to," Nick said philosophically, "and so does she."

"That's true." Amy strolled out to join them, looking incredibly beautiful in a soft summer party dress. "But we'll still have occasion to see each other when we want, maybe even baby-sit Dexter together again, after we pick up Lola and Chuck at the airport this afternoon.'' Amy floated closer, the wispy fabric of her sleeveless peach dress clinging dangerously to her slender curves. ''Take this evening, for instance.'' She smiled, all womanly invitation and reckless attitude. ''I've got a family party to go to for my long-lost aunt—and I don't have a date.'' She raised her chin in quiet challenge. ''What do you think, Nick?'' She flashed him a casual, reassuring smile. ''Interested in tagging along?''

It wasn't really a non-event. Nick knew that, even if Amy hadn't yet admitted it to herself. If he showed up with her at her family's party for Eleanor Deveraux, it would mean something—to both of them.

The question was, was he ready for that?

Because even if Amy just introduced him around as a casual friend, Nick thought, he and Amy would know what the truth was. They'd made love. And had he not been so intent on not hurting her or leading her on, if they hadn't had baby-sitting or airport pickup duty, they'd be in the bedroom again right now, making love again. Erotically. Dangerously yet tenderly.

And that was a risk.

Because if Nick didn't know better, he would think he was falling in love with Amy. He'd suspect she was already in love with him.

But he did know better.

And he knew Amy deserved more than he could offer. She didn't need a man like him. She needed someone she could count on. A man without demons.

On the other hand, he argued rationally, what was one more night? Or a favor returned? Amy had certainly gone all out, helping him with his extended family this week. Wasn't it time he helped her with hers, even if by only running interference between her and her trio of overprotective brothers?

"You're sure it would be okay, me tagging along tonight as a casual friend?" Nick asked, letting Amy know in a roundabout way just how he wanted to be regarded by her nearest and dearest. As no one special in her life. He stopped rocking abruptly and shifted a suddenly squirming Dexter a little higher in his arms. "Sometimes these family do's are just that—strictly family."

Amy smiled and reached for Dexter. She held him in her arms, and he stopped fidgeting immediately. "I think it would be fine," she said, dazzling Nick with a smile and looking more relaxed and trouble-free than ever. "Truth be told, both my aunts have little crushes on you."

To AMY'S PLEASURE and relief, the private jet carrying Chuck and Lola, along with the military medical personnel, was right on time. Lola came out first, then the stretcher carrying Chuck. For someone who had been through as much as he had in the past week, Amy thought, Chuck looked remarkably healthy and happy to be home—even if he couldn't yet stand up and walk on his own. Smiling broadly, Amy and Nick closed the distance between them.

Lola was sobbing openly with joy as she plucked her baby boy out of the stroller. "Dexter, Mommy has missed you so much!" Lola said, hugging him fiercely.

Dexter gurgled happily and grabbed two fistfuls of Lola's hair.

Tears still streaming down her face, Lola carried Dexter over to his daddy. She set Dexter down gingerly on the stretcher beside his father and, keeping a tight hold on Dexter, said, "Chuck, this is your son. And, Dexter, this is Daddy."

Tears leaked out of the corners of Chuck's eyes as he took his son's fist and kissed the back of it, then took him all the way in his arms and laid him across his chest so Dexter was facing Chuck. Dexter lurched forward in excitement and clapped his chubby little hands on Chuck's face, neck, shoulders. Chuck shifted him higher, and Dexter pressed his face to Chuck's. And the two of them stayed like that, nose to nose, eye to eye, for several minutes, Dexter cooing happily the whole time, Chuck weeping with joy and telling Dexter how much he had wanted to come and see him, how glad he was to be home.

"Thanks so much," Lola said, hugging both Amy and Nick, while Dexter and his daddy continued their very first meeting. Her voice caught and she continued thickly, "I would never have made it through this week without the two of you."

"You're welcome," Amy said. The week had not only been immensely enjoyable and educational, it had made her more aware than ever of her own need for a child and family of her very own. She wasn't sure if Nick was ready to admit it or not, but she knew that deep down he felt the same way she did.

"It was our pleasure," Nick agreed.

"Lola was worried," Chuck said as he shifted Dexter to his left side and reached over to shake Nick's hand. He gave Nick an assessing man-to-man glance that, Amy thought, spoke volumes about what Nick had been through years before. "But it looks like you and Dex and Amy all did okay," Chuck said, grinning.

They'd done more than okay, Amy thought. They had done wonderfully. Nick might not know it yet, she thought confidently, but he had proved that his yearning for kids was not as much a thing of the past as he had thought. Could his yearning for a wife and family of his own be far behind?

THE FAMILY REACTION to Nick, when he and Amy arrived at the party at her aunt Winnifred's, was pretty much just what he'd expected, Nick thought. Her brothers were cordial but regarded him warily, their three wives were a tad friendlier, though perhaps because of things their husbands had said about him, still cautious. Her two aunts, Winnifred and Eleanor, couldn't stop smiling at him. Grace was as friendly as ever to Nick, in a business-casual rather than familial way, and Amy's father, Tom Deveraux, seemed to be sternly assessing him and his attentions. To the point that Nick thought that if he hurt Tom's daughter in any way, the man would make sure there was hell to pay.

Not, of course, that Nick had any intention of hurting Amy.

He'd been honest and forthright with Amy from the very beginning. He would continue to be. He knew they wanted different things out of life. But for the first time, he was hoping they could compromise—find some middle ground. Find some way to be together without sacrificing everything they needed to remain happy or demanding literally everything from each other. Maybe, Nick thought, as he watched Amy circulate through the crowd, laughing and talking with each of her brothers and their wives in turn, there was a way they could meet each other halfway.

"So your brother-in-law is back safe and sound," Aunt Winnifred said, looking pleased about that, while beside her, Harry replenished the champagne glasses and buffet table, which was crammed full of Southern delicacies such as marinated shrimp and grits, crab cakes, Vidalia-onion casserole, spinach salad, cold spiced fruit, lemon chess pie and pecan brown-sugar pound cake.

Nick nodded happily. "Yes, he has more hospitalization and physical rehabilitation ahead of him at the military hospital here, but they expect him to make a full recovery. In the meantime, he gets to see a lot of his wife and son. And I think they're all looking forward to that." Eager to keep the conversation away from the topic of him and Amy and his intentions toward her, Nick looked at Eleanor and said pleasantly, "Speaking of hospitals, I heard you were recently a patient in one."

Eleanor shrugged and waved a delicate hand, as if it was nothing. "I sprained an ankle, had a touch of pneumonia."

"But you're all better now," Nick said.

"Except for this damnable chair." Eleanor pointed to the wheelchair she was sitting in, then flashed him a sassy smile. "But I'll be out of that before you know it, as soon as my ankle heals completely in another two weeks."

"YOU'RE LOOKING TENSE this evening, Dad," Amy said after dinner, when she found her father alone on the piazza.

Tom sent her a level look and said bluntly, "Maybe because I'm worried."

Sensing another lecture about protecting her heart coming on—she'd had half a dozen of them so far this evening, albeit discreetly—Amy tried a different tack. She tried to avoid the subject altogether by deliberately misunderstanding what her dad had been about to say. "You shouldn't be worried, Dad. Mom is staying in Charleston. Permanently. It hasn't been publicly announced yet," Amy rushed on before he could interrupt. "Only the preliminary papers have been signed, but she's going to have her own syndicated television show. Nick's company is going to produce it. And best of all, one of her stipulations is that it is going to be filmed right here in Charleston.''

"I know.'' Tom nodded. "Your mother told me."

Amy blinked. "Then why aren't you happier? Don't you know what this means?'' she whispered, frustrated her father could be so obtuse. "This is a sign that Mom wants to be near you and get back together!''

Tom rubbed wearily at the back of his neck. "She's dating someone else, Amy.''

Amy pooh-poohed that with a wave of her hand. "Her relationship with Paulo means nothing. They're just friends.''

Tom raised a brow and regarded Amy skeptically. "Did your mother tell you that?''

"Well, no…'' Amy shifted her weight uncomfortably from foot to foot. "But, Dad, it's obvious. He's so much younger than she is. And he's not at all her type.''

Tom put his hands on Amy's shoulders, wordlessly advising her to simmer down. "Amy, I know how you like to romanticize everything,'' he explained with a great deal more patience than he really seemed to feel, "and that's great when it comes to your work, because your decorating jobs are amazing. They're always right on the mark.''

Except with Nick's office, aka home, Amy thought. She was still—unhappily—in the process of redoing it, because she hadn't given Nick at all what he wanted, even if he was too considerate of her artistic sensibilities to come right out and say so.

"But there is no hope of a reconciliation between your mother and me," her dad continued bluntly. "The differences between us are just too great."

Amy sighed as her secret hopes for renewed family unity, instead of divorce and discord, were dashed all over again. "What you really mean is that Mom won't consider it," she presumed sadly.

"Neither of us will consider it," Tom corrected. He looked at Amy steadily, then continued, "Our divorce was mutual, Amy. We both realized our marriage was over. We both wanted it to end. We could not have gone on the way we were, hurting each other and you kids like that."

"So you split for the benefit of the whole family," Amy said in a discouraged voice, having heard that fact recited to her many times.

"Yes. And you should know something else, Amy," Tom said sternly, "now that we're talking about this as adults. I don't regret walking away from your mother. It was what she needed at the time, what we both needed. It was the only way back then that we saw to survive."

Amy saw the pain and regret in her father's eyes. "Would you do it again?" she asked, needing to know, even if it wasn't the answer she wanted. "If you had it to do over, would you make the same choices?"

"About your mother and me leading separate lives at that point in our lives?" Tom nodded soberly, his conviction about that much clear. "The answer is yes."

# Chapter Thirteen

"That must have been some talk you had with your dad," Nick said as he parked his car in front of Amy's home and cut the motor with a decisive snap of his wrist. "You've hardly said anything since."

"Maybe because I just came down to reality for the first time in my life," Amy admitted ruefully as Nick lifted her suitcases out of the trunk and carried them up the sidewalk. And although Amy was sad about that, because it meant she was going to have to change the way she'd been thinking for so many years, she was also relieved. It was time, she thought, to begin a new phase of her life. One that included Nick. And it was because of Nick, she thought, that she was finally able to view things more realistically, less idealistically. She unlocked the front door and led the way into the house, switching on lights as she went.

Nick followed her back out to the mailbox at the curb. "By realizing your family is still as wary as ever of the idea of you and me spending time together?''

Amy smiled, aware it felt good to be home after the week at Lola's cottage, baby-sitting Dexter. She plucked the day's mail out of the metal box and tilted her face up to his. ''Not everyone feels that way,'' Amy reported happily, knowing that it wasn't that her family didn't like Nick. They were simply afraid he would live up to his reputation and continue to avoid like the plague marriage and or serious involvement with a woman.

Amy made a teasing face at Nick as she related, ''My two aunts are cheering us on. Even Harry, Aunt Winnifred's butler, had something encouraging to say to me on the subject.''

Nick grinned and reached around behind her to close the mailbox door. His arm felt warm and strong as it brushed against her back, and to Amy's delight, he left it curved protectively around her as they started up the walk.

''Which was…?'' he prodded.

Amy shook her head, remembering, as she and Nick moved through the front entryway again. ''It was something like, 'You go, girl!'—which was pretty funny, coming from a buttoned-up Brit like him, but sincere, nevertheless.'' Amy slanted Nick a glance as she set the mail down on her living-room coffee table. ''He really wishes us well.''

Nick drew her close and pressed a kiss to her hair. ''Good for him—and us.''

Delighting in the impromptu show of affection, Amy wrapped her arms around his waist and hugged Nick back. "I thought so, too." She didn't know why it meant so much more to her, but she just knew Nick had a way of comforting her that was so much more meaningful and effective than anyone else's.

"But back to your unusual silence," Nick said as they moved apart again.

Feeling suddenly as if she had to move around or perish, Amy plucked up her antique watering can from its place beside the fireplace and carried it back to the white enamel sink in her country kitchen. Aware of Nick's eyes on her, she turned on the cold water spigot. "I told my dad about the deal my mother is making with you and your company, and that Mom has decided to stay and work in Charleston permanently."

Nick braced a hip against the counter and continued watching her. "And?"

"He already knew, and although he was happy for my mother—" Amy paused to turn off the water and lift the can out of the sink "—he didn't feel her presence here in Charleston was going to change anything between them."

Nick stepped back to allow her room to water the African violets on her windowsill. "And you had hoped otherwise," he presumed as they moved through the downstairs rooms, her watering plants as they went.

"Ever since they split, when I was fifteen, I have

done nothing but hope they'd get back together," Amy admitted as she tended to the last of the house plants on the first floor. "Now, finally, I know it's not going to happen."

"And that makes you sad," Nick guessed as he followed her up the stairs to the second floor's thirsty plants.

"I think they're throwing something very special away. And yet…" Amy paused as they entered her bedroom, bit her lip.

Nick searched her face. "What?"

"It's a relief to me, too," Amy admitted softly. She swallowed hard, before forcing herself to move on and finish her watering. "I guess I no longer feel like I'm personally responsible for their happiness."

Nick remained in the doorway, arms folded in front of him, one brawny shoulder wedged against the frame. "What do you mean?"

Amy shrugged and, finished with her task, moved toward him. "All my life I've felt responsible for other people's happiness in some way." She caught Nick's puzzled look as they moved back down the stairs to the living room. Wanting him to understand both the good and the bad things about her, she put the watering can back where it belonged and continued explaining herself to him. "I realized tonight maybe it's time I finally gave up the role of family peacemaker, and just let whatever is going to be, be." She linked hands with Nick and took comfort in both the affection in his eyes and the warmth and steadiness of his grip.

Nick pulled her close and wrapped his arms around her. "That's a pretty big decision." He stroked a hand lovingly over her hair.

"Also an empowering one," Amy said. She wrapped her arms around his waist and rested her face against his chest. She loved the way he smelled, a combination of soap and aftershave and mint. "Because if I no longer have to worry about taking care of everyone else, I can concentrate on me." She drew back and met his eyes. "And what I want and need."

Nick's eyes darkened with desire. "And that is...?"

Amy smiled and went up on tiptoe, aware she had never felt this safe and secure. "This." They kissed lingeringly, sweetly. But to Amy's disappointment, despite her overwhelming passion—and need—for Nick, she was not able to switch gears and put the tumultuous events of the evening aside as readily as she would have liked. Figuring she would be able to relax more readily in more intimate surroundings, she took Nick by the hand and led him upstairs to the master suite. But instead of stopping at the bed, as Amy had planned, Nick guided her into her luxurious new bathroom.

She watched as he let go of her hand and looking like a man on a mission, began running a bath in her brand-new whirlpool tub. Secretly thrilled at the way he was simply taking charge of the situation and simultaneously amused by the single-mindedness of his actions, Amy asked dryly, "What are you doing?" Not that she had any intention of stopping him, whatever it was.

Nick shot her an affectionate look that upped her pulse another notch, then plucked a bottle off the marble rim and poured it beneath the spray until fragrant bubbles rose up in billowing clouds. Finished, he turned her so her back was to him. He put both hands on her shoulders and massaged them gently. "I'm pampering you the way you deserve to be pampered. Besides—" he turned her to face him once again and his glance moved over her with male certainty, provocatively taking in her breasts, hips, thighs "—I know you're dying for a long, inaugural soak in your new tub."

Amy couldn't deny that. She had not only been yearning to climb in and enjoy the luxury of a tub big enough for two, she'd been fantasizing all week about doing so with Nick. "And what are you going to do while I soak?" Amy teased as if she didn't already know.

"First," Nick said as she slowly and deliberately toed off her heels, "I'm going to help you undress."

Sounded good so far, Amy thought cheerfully as Nick stepped behind her and unzipped the back of her dress, then drew it slowly down her arms and her body. She curved her hands around his biceps, and he steadied her as she stepped out of the delicate material. He paused to light the candles Amy had scattered around the pink-and-white bath and flicked off the overhead lights. Amy was delighted to see that bathed in the soft glow of candlelight, the expanded and completely redone room was every bit as romantic—and luxurious and feminine—as she had envisioned.

Nick stepped behind her, his ruggedly masculine presence adding to the seductive ambiance. He unclasped her bra, eased it away from her and over her arms. Her garter belt, stockings, panties followed. Naked, Amy turned to face him. As he looked at her with tenderness and appreciation, whatever tension she still felt fled. She was, in fact, more than ready to make love, then and there. But it was clear, from the look on his face, that Nick was enjoying the anticipation too much to rush through their joining. ''Soak first,'' he advised gently as he bent and kissed her lips. His hands warmly cupped her breasts as he whispered huskily against her ear, ''And in a minute I'll join you.''

Nick helped her into the tub, smiling as she sank into bubbles up to her collarbones, then disappeared from view. Aware she had been looking for a man this wonderful all her life, Amy tingled expectantly. A few minutes later Amy heard her bedroom stereo start up. Soft romantic music filled the room. Letting it soothe her as much as the gently churning water, Amy laid her head back on the rim and thought dreamily about the passionate connection that was to come. It was another five minutes before Nick reappeared, barefoot, jacket off, a bottle of chilled white wine and two long-stemmed glasses in his hands. Amy smiled, appreciating his love of comfort in this regard, too. "I ought to invite you over more often," she teased.

Nick poured her a glass of wine and handed it to her, before pouring one for himself. And then, still making himself at home, he began to undress. Amy's mouth grew dry as she watched him slowly unbutton and remove his shirt. Her heartbeat picked up as he took off first his trousers, then his shorts. She could barely keep her eyes off his broad shoulders, and strong chest. Lower still, the evidence of his powerful desire thrilled her even more.

"Did I ever tell you what a fine physique you have?" she murmured as he set his glass of wine on the rim of the tub and climbed in to join her.

"No, but I figured you felt that way." Smiling, Nick eased around so he was behind her. He braced himself against the side of the tub, then pulled her close so her back was nestled against his chest, her bottom cushioned between his open thighs and pressing against his tantalizing hardness. Kissing the back of her neck, he wrapped one arm about her waist and held her gently. Amy closed her eyes, enjoying the feel of him, the sensation of being so wanted and cherished and appreciated. Together they sipped their wine and luxuriated in the feel of the warm, bubbling water rippling over them.

The melting sensation in Amy's belly spread until it engulfed her from head to toe and the only thing on her mind was loving Nick, and being loved in return. Determination coursing through her, Amy set her glass aside. Her pulse racing with anticipation, she turned so she was facing him and wrapped her arms about his neck. "I don't know what it is about you," she murmured, noting all over again how handsome he looked in the soft glow of candlelight, how gallant, "but you make me feel so bold." So womanly and alive.

"That's good." Nick set his glass aside, too, and pulled her closer, so the insides of her thighs were against the outside of his, and she was straddling his body. He smiled, encouraging her to go with her feelings. "Because I like you bold. And sweet, and every way in between."

He tugged her closer still, and their lips met in a firestorm of need, and then all was lost in the passion of the kiss. Amy couldn't touch him enough. Nor could he get enough of her. They caressed and stroked and loved each other, with lips and tongues and fingertips, giving each other whatever was needed, until they were both gasping, shaking, impatient for more. The next thing Amy knew she was arching against him and he was sliding into her in a long slow stroke. Shuddering her pleasure, she settled against him, cloaking him in tight, wet, silky warmth. Trembling with a need they no longer wanted to deny, they rocked together, surging toward the outer limits of their control. And then there was no more holding back. No more restraint. Love and need swept through her, and then they were both climaxing and rocketing over the edge. And Amy knew the culmination of her dreams was closer than ever.

AMY AWOKE to the sight of Nick coming into the bedroom, tray in hand. Clad only in a pair of plain gray boxer shorts, he looked every bit as loved, rested and happy as she did. And she knew why. He had spent the entire night with her, making love—and then sleeping—in her bed. This time he hadn't moved away from her. Or once again resurrected distance between them. This time he had chosen closeness and intimacy over solitude. And that had to feel good to him, Amy thought. As good as it felt to her.

Happiness bubbling up inside her, Amy stretched languorously beneath the sheets. The smooth cotton brushed her bare skin as she yawned sleepily and struggled to sit up. "Breakfast in bed?"

"You're in luck." He waggled his eyebrows at her playfully, then set the tray down on the nightstand and leaned over to prop two pillows comfortably behind her. "Scrambled eggs and toast are the one thing I know how to make."

Stunned to realize she had never felt more cared for or more optimistic about her future than she did at that very moment, Amy noted he had made more than enough for two. "And coffee and juice, too. Mmm." She took a sip of juice and stirred sugar and cream into her coffee. "I could get used to this."

"Me, too." Nick munched on a triangle of toast.

"I haven't had a lazy morning in a long time. I forgot how good it feels."

He had forgotten, Amy thought, how good a lot of things felt. Especially, how it felt to be loved. But she could change all that. She put her fork down and looked at him seriously. She knew he was used to being alone. To not having a future in his personal life. But the time for punishing himself was over. And it was time he realized that and got on with his life and let himself love again. "Move in with me, Nick," she urged him quietly as she took his hands in hers. "Don't go back to living in your office. Stay here. With me."

The minute she said the words she felt him tense, and knew they were a mistake.

Nick frowned and moved his hand from beneath hers. "Amy…"

She ignored the awkward silence that had fallen between them and pushed on urgently, not about to back down now. "Last night was wonderful, wasn't it?" she asked eagerly, wanting, needing him to admit this was so.

"Yes." Nick forked up some egg and chewed it mechanically. He swallowed, took a sip of juice. And looked as if he was braced for the very worst. "It was."

Amy felt her customary optimism pushing through the fear, urging her on. "And you broke your rule, Nick," she continued softly, persuasively. "You didn't just get up and leave after we made love. You slept with me all night.'' They had awakened, wrapped in each other's arms, their bodies intimately and warmly entwined. Made love again in the dawn's early light and fallen back asleep.

Sometime after that Nick had gotten up and left her—but only to make her breakfast, not to escape the new closeness, the love they had found.

"And let's not forget I brought you breakfast in bed,'' he quipped, his mood visibly lightening.

"It's a great breakfast,'' Amy said enthusiastically, accepting the forkful of perfectly scrambled egg he offered her.

Nick took a bite for himself, then offered her another. "Yes,'' he said, his manner relaxed, but guarded, "it was.''

"So why can't we keep doing this?'' Amy asked, reaching over to lovingly feed him a triangle of toast. She knew how hard this was for him, and she intended to make it as easy and unthreatening as she could for him. But she needed him to take the next step. To tell her he loved her and wanted to be with her, even if he wasn't quite willing to move in with her just yet.

Nick's lips tightened. He sipped his coffee. "I'm willing to meet you in the middle.''

Amy regarded him, her heart brimming over with love and tenderness. She had an idea where he wanted to take this conversation, but she refused to give up hope, after all they had shared. "The middle being…?''

His tone gentled, turned more pensive and self-effacing. "I'm willing to commit to you, to give you my heart, to have us see each other exclusively from now on," he said, kissing the back of her hand.

"But you're not willing to live with me or marry me," she guessed. "Not now," she deduced, even more quietly. "Not ever."

Nick tensed, not about to lie to her. He swallowed, his eyes reflecting the depth of his regrets. "I'm not cut out for that, Amy," he said quietly.

"I want kids of my own, Nick," she told him, hanging on to her composure by a thread. She paused, feeling as if her heart was breaking as she searched his face. "I thought—watching the way you were with Dexter, how much you enjoyed rocking and holding him and caring for him—that you were beginning to want to have a family again."

Nick was silent, his expression tense and unhappy. Which was, Amy supposed, all the answer she would ever need. "You're never going to want what I want, are you?" she said quietly, pushing the breakfast tray away.

"Not everything, no." Nick caught her hand in his before she could leave the bed and guided her around to face him. "Which is why I'm willing to meet you halfway," he explained gently as he tugged her close and stretched out beside her. "I don't expect you to live with as few personal ties or commitments as I have been living for the past eleven years. Or sacrifice all your dreams just to be with me."

Amy rolled onto her side and clutched the sheet to her breasts, wishing belatedly she hadn't let herself be so vulnerable to a man who, she had known from the very beginning, was wrong for her. "But you do expect me to give up the idea of kids and marriage, for now, if I'm going to be with you in the short term, and for the rest of my life, if I want more than just a fling."

"I don't know how to answer that," he said, for a second looking as conflicted and vulnerable as she felt. "I never thought I'd want to spend the night with you, all night, in your bed. To be involved with or want to see only you, but I do. So maybe—" he shrugged his shoulders indifferently "—in time, I'll—"

"No, Nick." Amy swallowed hard around the gathering knot of emotion building in her throat. She knew where this was going, and after the night she had just had with him, the week, she didn't think she could bear it. "Just stop right there." She put up a staying hand as she slipped from the bed. Her back to him, she pulled on her robe to cover her nakedness and knotted it securely at her waist. Tears burned her eyes as she said huskily, "I really don't want to hear any more."

Nick got slowly to his feet. His gray eyes grim, he squared off with her. "I thought you wanted me to be honest with you."

Amy swallowed and blinked her tears away. In a panic at the prospect of seeing everything they'd found just swept away, she edged closer. The lack of understanding in his eyes was as chilling as the thought of a life without him. ''I also want you to be honest with yourself,'' she said huskily.

''I am.''

Amy took in the brooding expression on his face, the stubborn set to his jaw. She had to make him see what he was doing before it was too late. ''No, you're not,'' she retorted just as implacably. ''You're the kind of man who always knows what he wants, Nick, and nothing stops you from going after it. Take the situation with my mother.''

He shook his head at her and said in a low, censuring tone, ''That was business, Amy.''

''Which makes it perhaps the best example of your character, since business is such a huge part of your life,'' she said, choosing her words carefully. ''You wanted a deal with my mother, so you went after it, did and said whatever it took to get her to agree to do a show with her name on it with your company.''

''So?''

Amy studied him, taking in the short, sleep-tousled layers of his hair and the ruggedly sexy morning beard on his face. ''So my mother wasn't satisfied with just that,'' Amy explained tiredly. ''She wanted you to personally produce the show, which you haven't done in a while. And she wanted the show to be filmed in Charleston, which meant you would have to live here at least part of the time. Did that bother you?'' Amy asked emotionally, aware how hurt she was, playing second fiddle to the demands of his work. "Did that make you bat an eye? No," Amy rushed on, without waiting for Nick to reply. "Minutes later you were asking me to help you find a commercial Realtor to find you a place where you could work and live. And as soon as that was done, you wanted me to decorate the new space for you in less than a day!" Amy concluded, aware that much change, so quickly, in most people's lives, would have been enough to make their world spin.

Nick released an impatient breath of air. "What does all that have to do with us?" he demanded irritably, shoving a hand through his hair.

"The point is, you had no problem making any of those changes to your life even on very little notice." Amy forced her eyes from the hardness of his chest and the braced stance of his long muscular legs. "The only problem you had was when I made your new office-cum-sleeping place a little bit too homey for your taste. *Then,* you protested. Because you don't want a home, Nick," Amy recalled sadly. "So everything in that office had to go—"

"I never asked you to do that," Nick interrupted heatedly. He pushed the words through his teeth. "I would have lived with it, as is, and I told you that."

But that wasn't what Amy wanted, either. Nick living in less-than-ideal circumstances. He had already done that to disastrous effect in his early life. As an adult, he deserved, needed more. "My clients don't get less than what they need or want, Nick," she said stiffly. "I'm in the business of pleasing people. And that includes you. If I had just let it go as is, knowing you were secretly unhappy, I'd have to chalk that job up as a failure. And I couldn't have that."

"Which is why you went ahead and began redoing it even after I told you not to bother," he said irritably.

Amy shrugged, not about to take the entire blame for this fiasco, even as she admitted coolly, "I heard from my mother that you were caught off guard when you arrived—after I left there yesterday—for a meeting with her and found your office space empty again." Grace had pulled Amy aside at the party and suggested Amy not stun Nick like that again if she wanted to keep him for a client and friend. At the time Amy had figured she would just talk to Nick about that later when they were alone. But she'd never gotten around to it. Until now.

"But not to worry," Amy continued stonily, "office and living quarters will all be decorated—to your satisfaction this time—by the end of business today. Everything is already set for that." She had, in fact, intended to surprise Nick with a decor that was much more to his liking. "All you have to do is clear out and give me room to work."

"What does any of that have to do with us continuing our affair?" Nick asked, exasperated. He compressed his lips into a thin line. He braced his hands on his hips and glared down at her.

"Because that's all it will ever be—an affair,"

Amy said sadly. She paused, took a careful breath. "And because I know now, I've always known, I want more out of life than that. I just thought I could make you see the light. Make you realize you want the same things I do," she said miserably. "But you don't, do you, Nick?" she stated softly, looking him straight in the eye. "You don't want to be a husband and father, even though you'd probably be a great husband and father. You'd rather be alone. Well, you got it." She strode to the door and flung it open.

"What are you doing?" he asked.

Feeling as if her heart would never be whole again, Amy gestured broadly in the direction she wanted him to go. "I'm throwing you out of my home and my life. Because our love affair is over, Nick," she said evenly. "It's over and it never should have been started."

# Chapter Fourteen

"Something happened between you and Nick Everton, didn't it?" Eleanor asked the moment Amy walked into the carriage house to put the finishing touches on the new decor.

"I can see it too, darling," Winnifred Deveraux-Smith said, giving Amy a sympathetic look. "Thirty-six hours ago, you were here with Nick, and all Eleanor and I had to do was look at the two of you to know you were in love. Now, well, it's obvious something has happened to drive the two of you apart. Otherwise, you wouldn't be looking so sad."

It was true, Amy thought as she centered a lovely oil painting above the antique secretary desk. She did feel more bereft than she had ever felt before. And it was all because of Nick. Amy added a crystal vase to the table next to the sofa, then turned and regarded her aunts grimly, figuring if any two women could understand what she was about to say, it would be them. "I had hoped when I saw Chase, Mitch and

Gabe all get married to the loves of their lives this last spring, that the curse that has haunted our family for generations was finally going to be a thing of the past. But it's just not so.'' Amy plucked up a sweet-grass basket, made by local tradespeople, filled it with a stack of home-and-garden magazines and set it next to the hearth. Aware that the satisfaction she usually felt when successfully completing a job was not there today, she said, ''The Deveraux legacy of failed love lives on, after all. This time, through me.''

''Nonsense,'' Eleanor said, frowning. She patted the sofa next to her and motioned for Amy to sit down beside her.

Winnifred waited until Amy had complied. Then she sat down on the other side of Amy, took Amy's hand in hers and patted it gently. ''Your chance for happiness has not expired, Amy. If ever there was a man crying out for the love of a good woman—specifically you, Amy—it's Nick Everton.''

''I agree,'' Amy said, unable to contain her exasperation with Nick, her two matchmaking aunts and life in general a second longer. She vaulted to her feet, more aware than ever there was nothing anyone could say or do to comfort her.

Her heart aching, Amy said thickly, ''Nick does need me, even if he refuses to acknowledge it.'' She blinked back tears and began to pace restlessly. ''But I am through trying to fix up men the way I fix up houses,'' Amy announced self-effacingly as she went back to her work once again. ''I did that once, with

Kirk, and wasted five long years of my life.'' She shook her head. ''I am not going to be foolish enough to do it again with Nick. The changes he needs to make for us to be together are changes only he can make.'' Amy sighed, no longer able to hold back her tears. ''As much as I would like to be able to do it for him, Aunt Winnifred and Aunt Eleanor, I just can't.''

TWO HOURS LATER, Harry Bowles ushered Nick into Winnifred Deveraux-Smith's mansion. ''You two ladies wanted to see me?'' Nick asked Eleanor and Winnifred Deveraux-Smith.

They were seated in the front parlor having tea. ''Yes, Nick dear, we did.'' Eleanor Deveraux smiled at him resolutely, in that moment looking a lot younger than her eighty years. ''We want to talk to you about our niece.''

Nick tensed. He had been afraid it was going to be something like this. But he hadn't wanted to refuse the invitation on the off chance Amy's two hopelessly romantic aunts had figured out a way to resurrect his love affair with Amy. Instead, it seemed they had brought him there to lecture him on the error of his ways. And he'd already had that talk from Amy. Nick hadn't appreciated it then. Hadn't he told Amy the way it had to be, for the two of them, from the very beginning? Hadn't he already made more concessions for her than he had ever expected to make? Why did she have to insist on trying to make him succeed where he had already proved that he couldn't?

"Amy and I aren't seeing each other anymore," Nick said tersely as he perched on the edge of the wing chair and balanced a cup of tea on his knee. And that hadn't been his decision. He would have been happy to continue as they were. It had been Amy, he recollected unhappily, who had walked away from him without a backward glance or a seeming regret for all they would be giving up if they never saw each other or made love with each other again.

Eleanor passed him a plate of cookies. "So we heard." She regarded Nick gravely. "We think the breakup is a mistake."

Winnifred smiled gently at Nick. "We also heard—from Amy's mother, Grace—what everyone in the television industry apparently knows, that you're not the marrying kind."

For good reason, Nick thought. He wasn't any good at it. And he would be damned if he would put Amy, or any children the two of them might one day have if it was up to her, in the kind of jeopardy he'd placed his previous wife and unborn child. No. Amy deserved better, Nick thought fiercely. A hell of a lot better.

Nick hadn't seen any harm in the two of them having a fling if it helped get them past the allure of the road-not-taken thing. Then, when he had actually made love to Amy and spent time with her, he hadn't seen any harm in extending that to an indefinite love affair, with their future to be decided somewhere down the road. But Amy hadn't been satisfied with that. She had wanted him to give more than he felt he could. And then flat-out left him when he couldn't and wouldn't comply with absolutely everything she wanted of him. And for that, Nick was still smarting. Maybe because he hadn't expected to ever feel such heart-wrenching pain again. "I don't discuss my past or my love life," Nick told the woman.

"Of course you don't. And you know why? Because you haven't forgiven yourself yet," Eleanor said sagely.

Nick looked at the elegant older woman with the silver hair and the probing eyes in stunned surprise. "How do you know that?" he demanded warily.

"Because I sensed tragedy in your eyes. And I made it my business to find out, with the help of the private detective Winnifred used to identify me, what that might be. We know about the fire that took your wife and unborn child, Nick. We know what a tragedy it was."

Shock held him momentarily speechless. "Then you know I'm culpable for what happened," Nick said angrily.

"What I know," Eleanor corrected, a mixture of sadness and regret on her elegantly-boned face, "is that for years I refused to forgive myself for mistakes I made early in my life. Mistakes that cost the person I loved and was to marry his life. So I know what it is to wear that pain like a cloak of daggers for years and years and years, Nick,'' Eleanor continued, her voice quivering.

Her eyes gleaming with unshed tears, Eleanor paused to steel herself, then went on. ''I told myself, of course, that I was sparing my family and friends undue amounts of pain by dropping out of sight and feigning my own death. I supposed, back then, that only by never daring to love anyone again could I protect those around me from more harm. But that's the funny thing about love and family, Nick,'' Eleanor continued gently. ''You can't simply wish them away. Any more than you can erase your feelings or your deep concern for them.''

Nick swallowed hard around the growing tightness in his throat as the guilt of the past came back to haunt him, stronger than ever. ''I've never pushed my sister Lola or her family away.'' And though he did not to this day have much of a relationship with his parents, it wasn't for lack of trying. They simply weren't interested in building stronger bonds, and after a while Nick'd had to accept that. Just as he'd had to accept that there were some things in his life he couldn't do as well as others. Period. Like protect his own wife and child from harm.

''Instead you've done something worse than forsaking your extended family,'' Eleanor Deveraux continued shrewdly, not about to let Nick off the hook until she'd said everything she had to say to him. ''You've denied Amy—and yourself—the love the two of you could have if only you were brave enough to forgive yourself for the mistakes of your past. And risk love again.''

AMY HAD JUST PARKED in front of the building where Nick had leased the office-cum-private-sleeping quarters when Daisy Templeton pulled up beside her and got out of the beatup VW convertible she was driving these days. "Hey, I'm glad I caught up with you," Daisy said. "I've got the rest of those photos I promised you."

"Thanks." Amy took the envelope and tossed it onto the front seat of her car. She would look at them later.

Her face flushed with excitement, Daisy continued, "I wanted to tell you I was going to be gone for a week or two, so if you call me for a job and I don't get back to you right away, it's not because I don't want the work—I do—I'm just not here to do it."

"Okay. I don't think I have anything that will need to be photographed before you get back, anyway." Amy glanced at the suitcases in the back of Daisy's car. "Where are you going, anyway?" she asked.

The relief faded from Daisy's eyes and was replaced by unhappiness and confusion. "Switzerland. Harlan Decker, that P.I. I hired, found out I wasn't born in Norway or adopted out of an orphanage there, like I've always thought," Daisy revealed grimly. "I was born at a convent in Switzerland to an unwed mother who didn't want my birth father to know about me."

Amy sucked in a breath, aware that must be a lot to take in. She'd had enough trouble just dealing with her parents' divorce. "Wow," she said.

"Yeah, I know." Daisy shook her head bitterly. "I can't believe my parents lied to me about that, but they did."

Amy regarded her friend compassionately. Although Daisy had a reputation for being reckless, wild and totally unconcerned about the effect her actions had on her adopted family, Amy knew Daisy was really very vulnerable and tenderhearted. "What did they say when you asked them about it?"

Daisy dug the toe of her thick-soled sandal into the sidewalk. "I haven't told them I found out about it yet," Daisy admitted uncomfortably, averting her eyes. Shrugging aimlessly, she looked back up at Amy. "I figured if they'd lie to me about that, they'd probably lie to me about why they did what they did, too. So I'm going over to talk to the nuns myself and see what I can find out."

Still absorbing all she'd been told, Amy pulled out the checkbook for her business account and wrote a check to Daisy, paying Daisy for the photos. As she handed it over, she warned, "The nuns might not be able to tell you anything, either. Confidentiality rules, you know."

"Yeah, I know, but I've got to try." Tears sparkled in Daisy's eyes. "I've got to find out why there've been so many lies and so much secrecy, Amy," she said in a low, tortured voice. "Otherwise, I'm never going to be able to go on with the rest of my life."

"Well, I wish you luck," Amy said. "And if there's anything I can do for you..."

"I'll call," Daisy promised. She paused long enough to hug Amy, then hopped back in her car and drove off.

Amy watched her friend go, then reached into her car and grabbed the stainless-steel banker's lamp she had picked out for Nick's desk. Her mood as low as it had ever been, Amy locked her car and went on upstairs. She used the key Nick had given her to let herself in the condominium. To her surprise, Nick was sitting in the black leather chair behind the sleek glass-and-forged-iron desk. The breath stalled in her lungs at the sight of him, and he looked as if he had been waiting for her. But a confrontation wasn't what Amy wanted. She felt they had said far too much to each other already. To the point she could not bear any more pain. "I can come back," Amy said hastily, already backing out the door.

"I'd prefer you stay," Nick said, his eyes serious. It was clear he had showered and shaved with care. His hair was neatly brushed, and he was dressed in a dark-blue suit and a shirt in a slightly paler hue. He looked handsome. Sophisticated. And ready to take on whatever needed taking on—specifically, her.

Amy swallowed, her heart beating double-time at the new determination in his eyes. "I think we've said all the things we need to say, Nick,'' she told him quietly.

''Well, I don't.'' He stood, walked across the room and closed the door behind them. Suddenly he was right behind her. Close enough that she could smell the tantalizing scent of his aftershave. Close enough that she could feel the warmth of his body.

Pushing the memory of the passionate lovemaking they'd shared from her mind, she turned to face him. ''All right, then,'' she said impatiently, aware that if they stayed this close, she'd end up in his arms again. She regarded him steadily, stunned at how hungry she had been for the sight of him again after just two days, and how hard it was to tear her eyes from him. She'd thought she was finished with him, and he with her, given their different life goals. ''Make it fast.''

Nick stepped closer and invaded her space, his voice so quiet she had to strain to hear him. ''You want me to cut to the chase,'' he said.

Amy swallowed around the sudden dryness of her throat, and against her better judgment—hadn't they hurt each other enough already?—said crisply, ''Yes, absolutely.''

''All right then.'' He caught her hand and tugged her close. They collided, hardness to softness, and he looked down at her, his eyes dark and intense. In a low steely voice, he said, ''Marry me.''

Amy blinked, sure she hadn't heard right. Her mouth trembled with the emotions that had prompted her to run from him in the first place. ''What?''

Nick wrapped his arms around her. "I love you, Amy," he said, all the tenderness she had ever dreamed of radiating from him. "I want to spend the rest of my life with you. I want us to have babies and a home and everything we've both ever wanted and dreamed of. And in typical Nick Everton fashion, I want what I want today. So let's not waste any more time apart. Let's get married as soon as we possibly can."

Tears flooded Amy's eyes. She had only to look at his face to know the words he spoke came straight from his heart. He really had put the past behind him and opened himself up to love again, and the possibilities that came with it. "Oh, Nick," Amy breathed, feeling as if all her dreams had begun to come true. She rose on tiptoe and, loving the solid warmth of him, hugged him back, hard. "I love you, too. So very much."

Nick lowered his head to hers and touched her lips with his in a soft, heartfelt kiss. Her spirits soaring, Amy returned the kiss, then wanting to understand, pulled away slightly, splayed her hands on his chest and asked, "But I don't understand what happened to make you change your mind."

Nick threaded his fingers through her hair and continued looking down at her as if she was the most wonderful woman on earth. "Exactly what you'd think," he told her with a grin. He tugged a straight-backed chair closer with his foot, sank onto it and pulled her onto his lap. Holding her tenderly, he continued, "I came to my senses."

"But how?"

Nick's lips curved ruefully as he confessed, "Your great-aunt Eleanor and aunt Winnifred had a little talk with me. They made me realize that I had been punishing myself, the way Eleanor had punished herself, for letting a loved one down. And that I had to forgive myself, just as Eleanor has finally forgiven herself, and move on. Because staying away from you would not protect either of us from getting hurt again or make me stop loving you. Any more than being with you would guarantee that we would get the happily-ever-after we both want and deserve. Bottom line—there aren't any guarantees in this life, Amy," Nick said soberly. He tightened his hold on her. "There's no insurance that can promise us a happy tomorrow. It's all one big roll of the dice. And for a very long time, I've been afraid to participate in anything but business." He lowered his head and kissed her slowly, thoroughly, then drew back and promised, "No more. Starting today, I intend to live life to the fullest. And that means letting you—and love—into my life. So—" Nick looked at her with quiet confidence and said in a rusty-sounding voice "—back to my original question." He paused to search her face. "Will you marry me, Amy Deveraux?"

Amy's heart overflowed with joy. "Of course I'll marry you." She ran her fingers through his hair and looked deep into his eyes. "And I'll do it right away, because I don't believe in wasting time, either.'' Amy knew her feelings about Nick were not going to change. The kind of love they'd found was meant to last forever. And as far as she was concerned, their forever started today.

# Chapter Fifteen

"This is the fourth wedding in our family in two months," Winnifred Deveraux-Smith announced as she handed Amy the lacy blue wedding garter. She smiled as Amy lifted up her petticoats and slipped it on. "I'd say the Deveraux family is on a roll."

"Definitely," Amy said as Grace helped her into her wedding dress.

"No doubt about it. Amy's wedding to Nick today takes care of our generation," Mitch's wife, Lauren, added, stepping back to admire Amy's ivory satin dress, with the portrait neckline, fitted bodice and full, flowing skirt and train.

"Now if we could just work on the above-fifty age group," said Gabe's wife, Maggie, handing Amy a pair of pearl earrings—something borrowed.

Chase's wife, Bridgett, smiled optimistically. "I totally agree. I think some matchmaking is definitely in order for the single ladies left in this group."

Winnifred held up a staying hand. "I'm very content with my life as it is, thank you."

"There's no doubt you have a full life," Lauren said appreciatively as she helped Amy situate her tiara amidst the upswept curls on her head.

"Or that your longtime butler, Harry Bowles, is devoted to you," Maggie added with a look at Winnifred as she carefully attached the veil to Amy's tiara.

"But we all still think you should have a husband, too, in your life," Bridgett said.

Amy agreed. Now that she was with Nick, the man she loved and was meant to be with, she knew how much better life was. "And I think Aunt Eleanor should be married, too," Amy said.

The eighty-year-old Eleanor frowned. "I'm too old for that. The time for that in my life has passed."

"Maybe not," Grace Deveraux said as she helped Amy fasten a strand of heirloom pearls about her neck, while Theresa Owens, Tom Deveraux's housekeeper, stood by with the bouquet. "Winnifred and I could certainly introduce you to some eligible men in your age bracket."

Eleanor blushed with a mixture of excitement and pleasure, demonstrating, Amy thought, that her great-aunt and long-lost family member wasn't so far beyond marriage, after all.

Bridgett piped up with, "Actually, introductions could be made for all three of you. I'm sure if we put our heads together, we can come up with a whole list of eligible men you don't already know!"

Grace shook her head. "I'm done with marriage."

"So am I," Winnifred concurred.

"But that doesn't mean we aren't deliriously happy to see you getting married, sweetheart," Grace said as she gave Amy a warm hug. "Because if there is one thing we all agree upon, it's that you and Nick are meant for each other."

"Here, here," Bridgett said, raising her iced tea in salute. Everyone else picked up their glasses in silent tribute to Amy and the happiness she had found.

"To Amy and Nick," Lauren said softly.

"May they have everything they dream of," Bridgett added.

"Because no two people deserve it more," Maggie concluded.

Everyone clinked glasses once more and Amy was still smiling when a rap sounded on the door. "You ladies about ready?" Tom Deveraux called from the other side of the portal.

In the chapel beyond, the music started.

Grace stepped forward and opened the door. She and Tom exchanged glances that were as full of familial love and tension as ever. Then Amy's three brothers swept in to claim the bridesmaids they were to escort up the aisle, and the ushers claimed Grace, Eleanor and Winnifred, who were all led up the aisle and seated in appropriate order. Amy stayed back with her father, waiting her turn.

"You look lovely, sweetheart," Tom Deveraux said. He looked at her, paternal pride shining in his eyes.

"Thanks, Dad." Amy made a show of straightening his black silk bow tie. "You look wonderful, too." In fact, in his tuxedo, he had never looked better. And the same was true of her mother, resplendent in her lavender silk, mother-of-the-bride dress.

"Your mother and I are very proud of you. You know that," Tom said emotionally.

Amy nodded, a lump forming in her throat. Her father didn't often tell her things like that, so to have him tell her now, meant the world to her. "I'm proud of you and Mom, too, Dad," she said softly. And although she would always harbor some sadness about her parents' no longer being together, she had accepted it as the way things were and given up on trying to reconcile them or convince them to do it themselves. They were adults, and quite capable of running their own lives.

Briefly, sadness flashed in her dad's eyes, but—as always—it was gone. "I know sometimes in the past," Tom said, "you've felt your mother and I didn't value marriage, but that's not so, Amy. Your mother and I both know that the love of your spouse and family is what life is all about." He tucked Amy's hand in the crook of his arm.

Amy swallowed, hard, realizing that her dad's regrets about the end of his marriage to her mother had to be all the more poignant on a day like today.

"So it's very important you cherish that and give your marriage—and Nick—all you've got," Tom went on tenderly. Letting her know with a glance that he and her brothers and the rest of her family had put any doubts they had initially harbored about her and Nick to rest. Probably because they had seen how happy Nick made her, and vice versa, and knew that the couple's devotion to each other was the real thing. "Because if you do that," Tom concluded sagely, "you won't be sorry, I promise."

It was good advice, Amy thought, as her father escorted her up the aisle to Nick. And she planned to take it to heart. Just as she planned to keep hoping that everyone in her family would find the kind of love she and Nick had found.

But this time, Amy thought, she wouldn't be involved in the matchmaking.

No. She would let things happen as they were meant to happen.

With whomever they were meant to happen.

And in the meantime, she had everything she had ever dreamed of. She had Nick.

NICK HAD SEEN a lot of beautiful women in his time. But none compared to Amy Deveraux coming up the aisle on her father's arm. She was an angel in white, with a beauty that flowed from deep inside her. He didn't know how he had managed to live without her. But he knew one thing. He was never going to be without her again. And he made sure she knew it— in the heartfelt vows they exchanged, in the way he kissed her at the ceremony's end.

Not to be outdone, Amy rose on tiptoe, looped her

arms around his neck and kissed him back until there was no doubt how she felt, too. Forever in love. And every bit devoted to him as he was to her. By the time they drew apart, the chapel erupted in cheers and laughter and applause.

Even baby Dexter, who was seated in the first pew, along with his mommy and still-recuperating daddy, was elated. He waved and kicked and cooed. And Dexter was still cooing when Lola and Chuck came through the receiving line at the rear of the chapel to pay their respects.

"Congratulations," Chuck, who was still moving a bit stiffly, said. He offered his hand to Nick and kissed Amy's cheek, while Lola kissed them both.

"We're so happy for you!" she said as she shifted her squirming son to her other arm. "Dexter, too."

Amy and Nick smiled and accepted their congratulations and warm wishes. Dexter snuggled with them both before moving down the line with his folks.

"So what do you think?" Nick said minutes later, after he and Amy were seated in the back of the limo bound for the reception. He pulled her close. "Are you ready for a little rascal of our own?" He couldn't think of anything he wanted more, and he knew Amy was equally determined to have a family. To the point they had dispensed with birth control several weeks prior and concentrated on just loving each other and planning the wedding. Which, by the way, had gone off without a hitch. A fact that was, to Nick's way of thinking, anyway, a harbinger of their future together.

Amy shot him a sly look, brimming with joy. "Absolutely!" Amy said as she put his hand to her tummy. She had wanted to wait until that evening to tell him, but now that he'd brought it up... She kissed him, warmly and thoroughly. "Congratulations, Nick," she said as she gave him an affectionate hug. "You're going to be a daddy."

\* \* \* \* \*

# $ **Saving Money** $
# **Has Never Been**
# **This Easy!**

Just fill out and send in this form from any
October, November and December 2002 books
and we will send you a coupon booklet worth a
total savings of $20.00 off future purchases of
Harlequin and Silhouette books in 2003.

## **Yes! It's that easy!**

### I accept your incredible offer!
### Please send me a coupon booklet:

Name (PLEASE PRINT)

Address                                                              Apt. #

City                          State/Prov.                    Zip/Postal Code

### In a typical month, how many
### Harlequin and Silhouette novels do you read?
❏ **0-2**                                    ❏ **3+**

097KJKDNC7                                                          097KJKDNDP

**Please send this form to:**
   In the U.S.: Harlequin Books, P.O. Box 9071, Buffalo, NY 14269-9071
   In Canada: Harlequin Books, P.O. Box 609, Fort Erie, Ontario  L2A 5X3

Allow 4-6 weeks for delivery. Limit one coupon booklet per household. Must be
postmarked no later than January 15, 2003.

Start the New Year off regally with
a two-book duo from

HARLEQUIN®

AMERICAN *Romance*®

*A runaway prince and his horse-wrangling
lookalike confuse and confound
the citizens of Ranger Springs, Texas, in*

A ROYAL
TWIST

by
**Victoria Chancellor**

Rodeo star Hank McCauley just happened to be a dead ringer
for His Royal Highness Prince Alexi of Belegovia—who had just
taken off from his tour of Texas with a spirited, sexy waitress.
Now, Hank must be persuaded by the very prim-and-proper
Lady Gwendolyn Reed to pose as the prince until the lost leader
is found. But could she turn the cowpoke into a Prince
Charming? And could Hank persuade Lady "Wendy" to let
down her barriers so that he could have her, body and soul?

**Don't miss:**

# THE PRINCE'S COWBOY DOUBLE
January 2003

**Then read Prince Alexi's story in:**

# THE PRINCE'S TEXAS BRIDE
February 2003

*Available at your favorite retail outlet.*

HARLEQUIN®
*Makes any time special*®